"Are you a ghost?" Gwen asked

The stranger smiled, his teeth glittering brilliantly white in the half darkness, making her heart trip. "Not a ghost," he said, stepping closer. "I think you'll find I'm very real."

Gwen didn't move away, *couldn't* move away.

"Want me to prove it?" the man continued.

Before Gwen could answer, she felt him grasp her fingers, bringing them up and pressing them against his cheek. "Aren't ghosts supposed to be cold?"

She nodded weakly, gauging the rough warmth of his skin. He was definitely not cold. In fact he was just the opposite. Hot. Magnetic. Seductive. Her fingertips scraped across the stubble on his cheek in a helpless, subtle caress.

Gwen had never felt so exposed—or so excited. At this moment she honestly didn't know if she'd make one sound of protest if this total stranger took her in his arms.

And it looked as if she was about to find out....

Dear Reader,

I am a Halloween junkie. I love being scared, and I love scaring other people. At my place we go all out—big haunted house, graveyard in the front yard, guillotine on the driveway. I have as many boxes of Halloween stuff in my attic as I do Christmas decorations.

So when Harlequin gave me the green light for a Halloween-themed Temptation novel, you can bet I was excited. But if I was going to do it, I wanted to do it right...meaning it had to have everything I love about Halloween and romance all mixed up in one tempting little package. And that's just what *Trick Me, Treat Me* is. There are costumes and quirky characters, a haunted inn, mistaken identity, amnesia, secret agents, gangster molls, arms dealers and even a few ghosts. Not to mention a lot of heat...

So grab your pointy hats, hold tight to those broomsticks and be prepared for a lot of fun. You're about to go on a wild ride....

Happy reading—and happy Halloween!

Leslie Kelly

Books by Leslie Kelly

HARLEQUIN TEMPTATION

747-NIGHT WHISPERS
810-SUITE SEDUCTION
841-RELENTLESS
872-INTO THE FIRE
882-TWO TO TANGLE
916-WICKED & WILLING

HARLEQUIN BLAZE

62-NATURALLY NAUGHTY

Leslie Kelly

TRICK ME, TREAT ME

TORONTO • NEW YORK • LONDON
AMSTERDAM • PARIS • SYDNEY • HAMBURG
STOCKHOLM • ATHENS • TOKYO • MILAN • MADRID
PRAGUE • WARSAW • BUDAPEST • AUCKLAND

This one's dedicated to all the talented writers
who've helped me so often along the weary writing road.
To Marilyn, Mia and Laurie, who've been there since day one.

To Camille and Jill, who are always willing to
drop everything and give me a quick read.

And to Julie, Janelle and Karen,
who helped me shape this idea from the start.

Long live the Plot Monkeys!

ISBN 0-373-69148-3

TRICK ME, TREAT ME

This edition published by arrangement with Harlequin Books S.A.

Visit us at www.eHarlequin.com

Printed in U.S.A.

Prologue

October, this year

FIFTEEN-YEAR-OLD Rosario Sanchez was destined to be the worst maid in the world. She hated washing floors, loathed vacuuming and would rather stick a spike in her eye than clean other people's toilets. She'd long dreamed of being a hairstylist. "I'd love to take some bleach to Angel Fuentes's head, so she'll look like the *puta* she is," she muttered.

But no. No classy hair salon job for Rosario. After high school, she would take her place in the family cleaning business, like a rich girl would take her place at a debutante ball. Rich she wasn't.

Generally, life sucked. Still, sometimes her after-school job had perks. Like now. She sat in a Chicago penthouse owned by a writer who'd spent the last year overseas researching horrible murders for his next bestseller. She peeked at his photo on the back of his latest book. "Mr. Winchester you are *muy delicioso.*"

He was hot, even if he was old—at least thirty. He had dark hair, chocolaty eyes. Tall and mysterious, he was a man to sweep a maid off her feet, like in that Jennifer Lopez movie.

She'd like to help him write a new kind of book. "Romance," she said. Fantasizing, she reached into a giant bag of potato chips. Crumbling a handful of greasy chips on to the front of her sweater, she moaned, "Come and feast on me you big, sexy man."

Rosario eventually picked the crumbs off, popping each one into her mouth with her fingertip. They *were* Lay's, after all.

Grabbing the remote, she glanced around and cringed. The penthouse looked like it had been the scene of a huge party. Probably because it had. Last month. The night Manuel Diaz had dumped her for that bitch Angel. "*Puta,*" she said aloud this time.

She'd have to clean the place eventually. But not for a while. Her mother trusted her enough never to check anymore to make sure Rosario was performing her after-school dusting, watering and mail sorting duties at the penthouse. It wasn't like it needed real cleaning with it having been empty so long. The owner wasn't due back until late January—three months. She had time.

Grabbing the remote, she settled in for an hour of soap watching. Before she could even turn on her favorite show, however, she heard the door open. And nearly wet her pants.

Mr. Winchester is home early!

"Rosario?"

Worse. "Mama?" She groaned, a long, low sound holding both terror and dismay. This was *definitely* worse than the owner coming home. He, at least, wouldn't smack her in the head with a purse the size of a suitcase, like the one Mama carried.

A long stream of invective—all in Spanish—spewed from her mother's mouth. Rosario knew enough of the language to pick out several words, the kindest of which were lazy and useless.

Then the door opened again and her grandmother walked in. From worse to catastrophic.

"Mr. Winchester comes home tomorrow! What do we

do?" Her mother sobbed in what Rosario considered pure melodrama.

Grandmama glared. "We get to work *now.*"

Rosario did. Thankfully, her mother soon got too wrapped in getting beer stains out of the living room carpet to yell at her anymore. She'd escaped, at least temporarily, into another room.

It was while halfheartedly scrubbing the office floor that Rosario found a pile of dusty-looking envelopes against a wall. Several pieces of unopened mail had fallen from the desk. Mail Rosario was supposed to deliver to Mr. Winchester's secretarial company. She'd forgotten. For...uh... weeks...surely no more.

The postmarks said the items were a year old.

As she rifled through them, she thought quickly, fighting back panic. "Sales circulars...that's okay...oh no, bills. Paid now," she muttered and thrust them into a garbage bag. That left a few personal-looking items, including a thick manila envelope with a jack-o'-lantern sticker on it. "Maybe he'll think it's for this Halloween." Her voice held a pathetic note of hope.

"What you are doing?"

Caught! "Some mail fell back here," she whispered.

Grandmama muttered a wicked-sounding curse that would likely result in black hairs sprouting out of Rosario's back. Or warts on her chin. *Again.* Then she stalked over and seized the mail. Sighing, she shook her head and raised her eyes heavenward, a picture of visual piety. "We leave it in God's hands."

Grandmama, however, apparently thought God's hands were full enough with piddling issues like world peace, the stock market and the prayers of hopeful lottery players. She seemed to want to help him out. Reaching into the bucket

Rosario had been using to wash the floor, she retrieved a sponge full of dirty water. Rosario watched, shocked, as her grandmother smeared the sponge over the exterior of the remaining envelopes.

"No telling when they came," the old woman said. "Lost. Ruined by bad weather. He throws them out himself. No blame."

Her grandmama was *helping* her? Not calling to Mama to come and deliver more shouts or bruising swings of her handbag? Rosario clutched her grandmother's skirt. "Thank you."

In response, she got a smack in the head with a wet sponge.

"You're fired."

1

A few days later

JARED WINCHESTER wished the weather was warm enough to merit the brilliant blue of the autumn sky. But in spite of the clear day—such a change from the dark Russian skies he'd seen for the past year—the temperature was brutal. Too bad. He'd have loved to put down the top on his convertible for the drive to Derryville.

He settled back in his leather seat, one hand on the steering wheel. God, he'd missed his car. Almost as much as he'd missed the sunshine.

His trip to research the Glanovsky serial killer case had come to an end a few months early due to interference from the government. But not early enough. He'd returned a couple of days ago just in time to go from freezing cold Russian autumn right into freezing cold Chicago winter. It'd been more than a year since he'd felt warm.

Perhaps it was appropriate, considering he'd soon be writing a book about one of the coldest crime sprees the former Soviet Union had ever seen. The Soviets hadn't liked to admit to such western aberrations as serial killers, so they'd done some covering up over the years. Jared had *uncovered* a lot. Enough that the present officials had gotten antsy and stopped cooperating. "Let it go," he murmured, not wanting to let frustration over bureaucracy affect his drive to his cousin's party.

With a tap of a button, the car filled with a blast of good old head-banging hard rock from the good old U.S. of A. His favorite music, though few would believe it. Damn, home felt good. Put a six-pack of real beer in the trunk, and a fast-food burger made of real beef in his hand, and he'd be set. It was time to reclaim his normal life. Get out of the world of a serial killer, at least until he had to begin writing the book he was contracted to deliver next spring. Beer and burgers would help.

"Some mind-blowing sex wouldn't hurt, either."

Not that he'd been celibate in Russia. He'd had a little fling with a detective who had a thing for cowboys. It had been fun, though she'd been disappointed that he'd refused to have sex while wearing boots and a ten-gallon hat. Not to mention spurs.

But it had been too long since he'd enjoyed slow, sensual sex with someone who liked to curl up together afterward. Martina, the cowboy groupie, had preferred to go arrest people after a hot romp. Jared was out of the arresting people business. Way out. And he had no interest in returning to it.

Since he had no serious woman in his life, and hadn't kept in touch with any of the less serious ones, that need would have to wait. The difficulty with relationships was one of the toughest parts of his job. Not just because of the travel, but because most women couldn't take what he did. The crimes he researched, his ability to reconstruct horrific events...well, he hadn't met a woman yet who'd even tried to understand. And the fact that he tended to be a pretty introverted guy could throw a woman off. He spent nearly all his time doing research and writing. His social skills were pretty rusty.

Sure, women understood the paycheck, the penthouse, the cars, the cash. But not the man. Never the man.

That probably wasn't too surprising. His own family had a tough time understanding the way his mind worked sometimes. When his parents had asked why he was leaving the bureau a few years back, he'd tried to explain. Being raised in a family of cops had made him develop a fascination with crime from a young age, even though Derryville hadn't exactly been crime central.

The fascination, however, wasn't so much in solving crimes, but rather in understanding the psychology behind them, in putting the pieces together to figure out not only what had happened, but *why* it had happened. And, perhaps, in preventing something similar from happening again.

That pretty much summed up why the FBI hadn't been for him, while writing true crime novels was.

Glancing at his open briefcase, he ignored the stack of files and photos from the Russian case, which he *should* have left at home. Instead he focused on the smeary padded envelope—the reason for this trip. "Mick, you are one crazy son of a bitch."

Leave it to his cousin to plan an outrageous Halloween party. A murder weekend. Complete with thrills and chills at a bona fide haunted house. Right up Jared's alley. *Time* had, after all, recently called him the Stephen King of the nonfiction world. As a big fan of King for years, he'd taken it as a huge compliment.

The key wasn't the murder, thrills and chills. Knowing Mick, this weekend would be pure fun. Low stress. And with Mick's love for practical jokes, a lot of laughs. Just what he needed.

The plans for the party were intricate. The envelope contained realistic-looking fake ID, and a dossier on his character. There were maps, coded messages, even a photo of the bad guy—an international arms dealer—he was allegedly pursuing.

Jared looked the part, too. He'd dressed all in black. And he'd found props, including a small, fake handgun that was really a cigarette lighter, and some stuff he'd gotten when researching a book on old Chicago organized crime—a side interest he dabbled in when he got the chance.

He kept thinking of his destination. The Marsden Place.

Mick had set up a scenario with a group trapped at a spooky inn for a weekend...in the old Marsden house, the scariest building in their hometown. He couldn't imagine a less inviting inn. Except on Halloween. Tonight it would be just about perfect.

Mick was a real estate agent. He'd been trying to sell the house for two years, since the former owner had died. But nobody with any common sense would want it. Talk about white elephants. It had needed tons of work a decade ago...he couldn't imagine how the house looked now. "Probably just right for a murder party."

Mick might be the theatrical one, but Jared was up for a challenge. His cousin's invitation had been a thinly disguised gauntlet. Since he'd known Jared was supposed to be gone until January, he was daring him to come home to Derryville early.

Derryville. Funny, he'd once considered his hometown a two-stoplight dump, from which he'd longed to escape. Somehow, his feelings had mellowed once he'd built a new life elsewhere. He'd enjoyed his few trips home over the years, even if he hadn't been able to resolve a few long-standing family issues.

A trill of his cell phone interrupted his thoughts. "Hello?"

"Jared! I didn't wake you, did I? Not sure what time zone you were in. Moscow—is that ahead of us or behind?"

He recognized the voice of Alice McCoy, his literary agent and friend. "Ahead. Eight hours. But it's okay, I've been home almost two days. And I've readjusted to all things American, except the tendency to supersize portions of absolutely everything." He sipped from a Super Big Gulp he'd picked up when stopping to gas up for the trip. "But I'm remembering why I like it."

"Well, I'm glad you're back. We've got tons to do."

A truck swerved too close from the other lane, nearly cutting Jared off the road. As he tapped the horn, he hoped his secretarial service had paid up his insurance. They hadn't done much else right—hadn't even forwarded his damn mail, for weeks.

Alice obviously heard the horn. He could almost hear the muscles of her face pull into a frown. "You're in your car."

She sounded as disapproving as his fourth-grade teacher, who'd liked to make him write, "I will not make up stories that frighten other children," a half-million times on the chalkboard.

"Yes."

"Why aren't you sitting at your desk writing this fabulous new book that's going to make you rich...*er?*"

"I'm taking a brief trip. Going to my hometown."

"Haven't you traveled enough?"

"It's my favorite holiday. Don't I deserve a break? I've been invited to a murder mystery party for Halloween weekend."

She laughed, her smoky voice thick from decades of cigarettes and expensive bourbon. "Right up your alley, so I guess you're allowed. Does your family know you're coming?"

He heard the unasked question. *Does your grandfather know you're coming?* "No." And it was probably just as well since his relationship with his grandfather had grown decidedly strained over the years. Another reason for accepting Mick's invitation. It was past time to mend that fence, to fix that broken relationship.

Jared had gotten friendly with a grizzled old Russian lieutenant over the past several months. On Saturday nights, Nicolai liked to drink vodka and reminisce about the family he'd lost because of his obsession with his career. Every word he'd spoken had reminded Jared that it was time to extend an olive branch to his grandfather before it was too late.

"You're going to show up unannounced?" She sounded surprised that her reserved client would do something so impulsive.

Yeah, it was slightly out of character, which was what he needed. "Actually, *I'm* not going to show up unannounced. Miles Stone, the secret agent who's a cross between James Bond, Austin Powers and Maxwell Smart is showing up unannounced."

Another low laugh. "Bond I get, given your looks."

He grinned. It wasn't a compliment. A disgruntled Alice had once told him he was much too good-looking to be taken seriously as a brilliant criminalist.

"And I guess you probably like women as much as Powers. But, I gotta tell ya, you're too young to remember, but I'm not. Maxwell Smart *wasn't* the best secret agent in the world."

"Which is why my obnoxious cousin mentioned him."

"Gotcha. Is that why you didn't RSVP? To get even?"

"Nah. Mick has no idea I'm back. He knew I was supposed to be overseas until after Christmas. He sent the invitation to taunt me about missing my favorite time of year. *Again.*" He smiled evilly. "He deserves to have a guest crash the party."

"Hope he doesn't kick you out of his house."

"It's not in his house. The party's taking place in the house of my childhood nightmares."

As expected, the bloodthirsty sixty-year-old, who loved his books, was immediately intrigued. "Tell me more."

After he had, she said, "Is your cousin in the habit of having private parties in the houses he's got listed for sale?"

Actually, he didn't imagine Mick would give something like that a second thought. "The house is in trust with a lawyer. I'm sure he got permission." Since he and Mick hadn't spoken in ages, Jared didn't know how he'd finagled the use of the house for the weekend. But he'd bet there was some back-scratching involved.

In Derryville, back-scratching was involved in every deal. From which fireman would drive the big rig for the Labor Day parade, to who got to flip the switch for the Christmas tree in town square, Derryville was a microcosm of the good old American barter system. It didn't trade in goods...just favors.

God, it all sounded so appealing. The very sameness, the normalcy that had made him long to escape years ago was exactly the balm his battered spirits needed right now. Home. It was so blissfully, soul-soothingly simple. Easygoing and peaceful. Exactly what he needed after a year of crazy but wonderful Russian cops, and just plain crazy criminals. Which is exactly what had made him decide to accept his cousin's invitation.

He could hardly wait for the weekend to begin.

"HURRY HOME NOW. It's after nine. Chief Stockton won't want to see any ghosts and goblins on the street so late."

Gwen Compton waved at one last straggling group of trick-or-treaters as they skipped across her front lawn. They laughed and yelled, kicking crunchy brown leaves out of the way in their haste to make it to just one more house before heading home.

The full moon cast gentle illumination on the road leading down the hill, so she didn't fear for the children's safety. The road wasn't busily traveled. Only their guests—all of whom were already settled in for the night here at the bed-and-breakfast—used it. The moon was aided in its quest to brighten the night by softly glowing streetlights, which had miraculously escaped the mischief night BB guns that had taken out many of those downtown.

She watched the kids dart from puddle to puddle of light, pausing beneath the lamps to grab one more bit of candy, to toss out the odd apple or exchange a lollipop for a jawbreaker. Probably all of them were jamming chocolates into their mouths in spite of their parents' dire warnings to let them check their candy before they ate it. In a town like Derryville, who could blame the kids? The only slightly scary thing about this peaceful Illinois place was the house in which she stood. Her home.

Shutting the door, she sagged against it and sighed, both relieved the evening was over, and also slightly sad to see it come to an end. Her first Halloween in the spookiest haunted house in town. *Her* home, which she adored—dark corners, scary turrets, strange creaky noises and all. And it had been a resounding success.

Of course, they probably wouldn't have a single guest for the rest of the year. But she knew when they opened last month that Halloween would be a sellout, given the house's reputation. They'd come close to meeting her prediction. Only two of their thirteen rooms remained vacant. That had proved fortunate. A broken pipe had caused a flood in her room, forcing her out. She'd have to stay upstairs for a few days.

"Aww, dangit, they're gone. Think that's it for the night?"

Glancing up, she hid a smile. Her great-aunt Hildy was peering out the window, looking mad enough to spit.

"I think so."

"Rats. I didn't make it outside in time to sing to that last group." The old woman shook her head. "Knew I shouldn'ta had that second frankfurter for dinner. I been in the bathroom half the night and missed mosta the fun."

Not particularly caring to hear about the bathroom habits of an old lady, Gwen turned to lock the front door.

"I still think I shoulda got that psycho killer mask and a chainsaw and chased the little devils down the hill."

"You would have fallen and broken your hip."

Her great-aunt shot her a look that demanded an apology. Gwen refused to give her one. Spry and in physically perfect condition or not, Hildy *was* eighty-five years old.

"You coulda done it," Hildy finally said. "The old Gwennie would have."

The old Gwennie. Hmm...Gwen remembered her. Sometimes she even smiled when she thought about that wild, free-spirited person who'd been hell on wheels as a teenager, rebellious and daring as a young adult. Who'd loved hack-em-up thriller movies, and had once dreamed of being in the FBI so she could outwit her own Hannibal Lechter.

Gone. Long gone. Somehow that person had become a quiet, rather sedate woman who ran an inn with her elderly relative and did nothing more exciting than occasionally go out without wearing a bra.

But that was okay. Everyone had to grow up sometime.

"I like this costume better on you, anyway," Gwen replied, not responding to Hildy's remark. She gave her great-aunt a visual once-over, studying the spiked, shocking-pink wig, and the thigh-high white patent leather boots sticking to the skinniest pair of old lady legs this side of a refugee camp. Combined with the glitter makeup on the woman's eyes, the red leather skirt, white spandex top and pink feather boa, Hildy made quite a picture. Seeing Aunt Hildy as a punk rocker had probably been more effective at giving kids nightmares than any chainsaw wielding maniac could ever have.

"Sam seemed to like it," Hildy said with a suggestive wag of the eyebrows.

Sam Winchester was Hildy's eighty-seven-year-old gentleman friend. He and Hildy had been "stepping out" together for a few months, which Gwen was glad about. Hildy might be too old to settle down, marry and have the children she'd never had, but she certainly wasn't too old for a little romance, a little happiness. Heaven knows she hadn't had much of either one in her life.

"Toldja no kids would recognize you as Glenda the Good Witch." Aunt Hildy rolled her eyes as she again examined Gwen's pink dress and the long ringlets she'd curled into her hair.

"But everybody's seen *The Wizard of Oz.*"

"Bo-o-o-ring. You gotta stop playing it safe. You're a hot tomato, sugar lips. You just need to get back to normal, be daring like you used to be."

She ignored the lecture on not playing it safe—lord knew, she'd been hearing it almost daily for almost two years, since her parents' untimely death had shocked her into a life of safety and solitude. The ugly public breakup with her former fiancé had also made her "tuck up inside her shell like a pansy-ass turtle," as her Aunt Hildy liked to say.

She didn't mean to play it safe. In fact, recently she'd begun trying to do at least one spontaneous, risky thing each day, even if it was only wearing a darker shade of eye shadow, or a thin, filmy blouse on a windy October day. *With* a bra.

She could also admit, if only to herself, that it probably was the old Gwennie who had fallen crazy in love with this dark, gothic-looking house from the moment she'd laid eyes on it.

"You should've dressed up as that singer Madonna," Hildy added. "Moe says you coulda superglued some of them big, pointy ice cream cones over your ta-tas and looked just like her in one'a her bustiers."

Gwen also ignored the ta-ta remark. She didn't want to think about the possibility of supergluing *anything* to her breasts. Particularly since the suggestion had been made by Moe. Her great-aunt's best pal. The dead gangster whose ghost currently made his home in their basement.

She supposed there were worse ways Hildy could spend her golden years than talking to the ghosts from her past. She was just thankful Hildy had lived to *see* her golden years. And that Gwen was around to take care of her and share them with her.

Hildy's family had disowned her when she was a disgraced teenager, having fallen in with a notorious gang of Chicago bank robbers back in the thirties. From what Gwen could gather, Hildy's own parents had done nothing to help her when she'd been thrown into jail, only grudgingly letting her come home after she'd served her three-year prison sentence.

Aunt Hildy's life hadn't gotten much easier once she was released. Never allowed to forget she'd disgraced the family, her sadness had led to deep depression, and eventually a nervous breakdown. She'd spent years in and out of mental institutions. Something Gwen still had trouble fathoming, considering Aunt Hildy had been a smiling, gentle presence through her whole life.

She put her arm around her elderly aunt's frail shoulders and gave her a gentle squeeze. Gwen was too grateful to have the slightly zany, but deeply loving old woman around to quibble over trifling matters like talking to a dead gangster. Hildy was the only family she had left. And Gwen would do anything to make her final years happy, tranquil ones. Anything to help Hildy forget that her family had once betrayed her.

"How would Moe know about Madonna?" she finally asked, knowing demonstrations of affection made Hildy uncomfortable.

"TV."

She turned out all but one light in the foyer, partially to prevent her aunt from seeing her amusement. "Of course. Moe loves TV, I remember." Personally, when she was in Moe's position, Gwen hoped television would have no part of her existence. A world without TV—no reality shows, no WWF smack-downs and no Jerry Springer—sounded like *heaven* to her. Then remembering the Madonna bustier suggestion, she added, "You know, those ice cream cones would break in no time flat."

Hildy thought about it. Finally, her eyes narrowed and her brow pulled into a frown. "That dirty old geezer. He always was..."

"Never mind, Aunt Hildy. I'm sure he didn't mean anything." No way did she want to get into a discussion about Aunt Hildy's former associates tonight. Yes, she'd loved the stories as a kid...the gorier the better. Hildy used to call her Gruesome Gwen because she'd been so fascinated by the wicked old days. She'd learned all anyone could know about prohibition, the benefits of a Tommy gun, how many men Pretty Boy Floyd had murdered and John Dillinger's penis size before her eighteenth birthday.

The penis size thing was *still* pretty interesting.

But she hadn't had time for stories since they'd moved here.

"All the candy gone?"

"Just about. I'm glad you insisted on buying so much." Gwen lifted the nearly empty bowl, casting a rueful eye to one lone piece of bubble gum and a few forlorn-looking Tootsie Rolls. "I never knew there were so many kids in Derryville."

Hildy tugged her wig off and patted a strand of white hair into her bun. "And every one of them *had* to come here."

Gwen couldn't count the number of times a group of children had come to the door tonight, looking uniformly terrified but so excited they couldn't stand still. Each time, they'd pushed forward one unlucky little soul to be their spokesman. The voice would tremble, the eyes would sparkle with fear. Eventually each would muster up the courage to whisper, "Trick or treat."

They'd peer around her, trying to get a look inside the infamous house, which had cleaned up rather well after months of work. Well enough to open their inn before the end of the year, as she and Hildy had hoped when they'd moved here last February.

"I'm bushed," Hildy said, rubbing at her hip, visibly fatigued. "You think you can close up for the night, sugar lips?"

Nodding, Gwen kissed the old woman's forehead, wishing she'd realized sooner that Hildy wasn't feeling well. "Go on." Hugging her aunt again, she took care to be gentle with those fine, delicate old shoulders, on which Gwen had leaned more than once as a girl.

As Hildy walked away, she said, "Don't forget to thaw out the muffins so they'll be ready for the morning."

"I won't forget."

But, of course, she did.

JARED REACHED Derryville very late, due to Friday night traffic on the interstate, but he didn't worry. This gathering was set to last the whole weekend. Besides, since he wasn't expected, it would be easier to slip inside—in character—to surprise his cousin. If he got the chance, he could manipulate the "evidence" and pin the crime on Mick. Guilty or not.

Mick deserved some payback for the Maxwell Smart stuff.

He cut off his headlights as he drove up the hill leading to the old Marsden house, not even fully realizing he was holding his breath as the imposing building came into view.

It hadn't changed. Dark and angled, it was an architectural monstrosity that had never fit in with the quaint midwestern town. It overlooked Derryville like a crouching dragon guarding its village for its supply of tasty virgins.

Several cars were parked in the lot at the side of the house, evidence of the party underway. The building appeared dark, so it was possible some people had retired for the night. Or, perhaps, they were busy being bumped off in Mick's game of "figure out who the killer is before you get murdered yourself."

Jared got out of the car after tucking his keys up behind the sun visor. As soon as he had a chance, he planned to come back and move his Viper into the garage. He also left the invitation and his wallet in the glove box, intending to be in character as of this moment. He didn't worry about anyone stealing anything. This was Derryville, after all.

As he walked to the porch, he noticed a small sign. Mick had gone all out, having a fake sign painted for his inn. In print, it didn't make much sense. Little Bohemie Inn. Spoken aloud, however... "Little Bohemian. Cute, Mick."

He paused at the bottom step. "Finally gonna get to see the inside," he murmured. His mind tripped back to long, restless nights when he'd lie awake in his bed, imagining the horrors buried beneath the floorboards of Miser Marsden's house.

What would old man Marsden say if he knew one of the town's most famous residents had used descriptions of his home in his earliest horror-writing efforts? The Marsden house, with its dusty turrets, so dark and imposing against even the sunniest summer skies, had definitely been inspiring when it came to writing spooky tales. But practically nobody knew about the stories, long buried in trashed periodicals or out-of-print slasher rags. Jared was now on the bestseller lists with nonfiction, not the dreck he'd tried to write while in college.

He'd never seen the inside of the house—though not for lack of trying. He and Mick had climbed the rickety outside steps up to the wide, creaking wooden porch to ring the doorbell once, years ago. They'd done it on a double-dog dare, to see if old man Marsden really did have a Doberman named Killer, trained to bite the nuts off any boy stupid enough to trespass on his property.

Marsden hadn't answered. Neither had Killer. Which left Jared with hope that he might someday be able to father a rugrat or two. He also hoped that if there were any ghosts in the Marsden place, Killer wasn't among them.

A dog howled in the distance and he had to laugh at his own start of surprise. Shaking off old memories, he put one foot on the step, then paused. Miles Stone, superspy extraordinaire, would never walk through the front door—or worse, knock.

Without another thought, he turned and made his way around to the back of the house. He'd just stepped through an unlocked back door when he realized he wasn't alone.

A figure in white—either a ghost or the most attractive female he'd ever seen—stood a few feet away. Jared froze, watching her move into the kitchen, unaware of his presence.

She was clad in a shimmering gown, and her golden hair was long and wildly curled against her curvy body. While she'd been silhouetted in the doorway, he'd gotten a glimpse of a sweetly soft face complete with full pouty lips. Every male instinct he possessed came to attention instantly in a way he hadn't experienced in a long time.

Remaining in character, Miles Stone prepared to do what any James Bond would do. Find out who she was. Remove any weapons she might be carrying.

Then get her into bed.

2

GWEN HAD REMEMBERED the muffins forty minutes after she'd gone to bed in one of the upstairs guest rooms. "Damn," she'd sworn at her absentmindedness. How could she have forgotten when Hildy had reminded her?

To give herself credit, she had been working awfully hard. Eighty-hour workweeks filled with ladders, paint cans, scrub brushes and sewing machines could drive every thought out of anybody's head. But it wasn't *anybody* who was going to have to oversee breakfast for their guests. It was *her* body.

Sighing heavily, she'd gotten up, wishing she'd thought to grab a bathrobe from her own room before coming upstairs for the night. Her thin negligee had done nothing to warm her. She'd made a mental note to stop to get the robe before coming back up.

In the kitchen, she hadn't bothered to flip on the blinding overhead fixture. The lamp in the hallway banished most of the shadows, and she'd left the small light over the stove on, as usual, in case Aunt Hildy needed something during the night.

Now she was inside the room—maneuvering around familiar cabinets and fixtures—and that was when she realized she wasn't alone. A man stood near the table. A man clothed all in black.

He remained motionless. A shadow. A phantom. A spectral memory of someone who'd stood there decades before.

She instantly thought of Hildy's ghost friends. When the shadow moved, separating from the inky blackness in the corner, she made out more of his features and gasped. "Good lord."

Not a phantom. Not a ghost. And, hopefully, not a maniacal murderer out and about doing his gruesome thing on Halloween night. Because he was very tall. Very broad. Very male.

"Don't be afraid."

Who wouldn't be afraid? Alone: check. Dark man in kitchen: check. Spooky house: check. Halloween night: *start screaming now.*

"Really, you have nothing to fear," he continued in a voice that was both soft and masculine, soothing and melodic.

Sure. Right. *Don't be afraid, I'm harmless, says the cobra to the little pink mouse.* Of course, the little pink mouse might drop dead of a heart attack before the big bad snake had a chance to even nibble on a whisker. She backed up until cornered against the countertop. "Who are you? What are you doing here?"

"I'm a guest at the inn for the weekend."

Her whole body began to relax. "A guest?"

Of course. Hildy had checked in several people today. Gwen obviously hadn't met everyone. She nearly chuckled at her own foolishness. No ghost. No ax-wielding maniac. Just a paying guest. She wasn't used to the fact that they were an open, operating inn, and she and Hildy were no longer alone in this huge, ghostly house. "Good lord, you scared me half to death."

"I'm sorry." He stepped closer, until more light from the hall spilled on to his face. His deep-set brown eyes glittered in the near darkness. Simply mesmerizing.

Then he stepped even closer until his entire face was visible. She caught her breath, held it, then released it on a sigh, knowing she'd never seen a sexier guy in her life.

Each female molecule in her body roared to awareness, reacting to the male sensuality oozing from his body. His cheekbones were high, his chin firm and chiseled. His thick, dark brown hair was a little long, and his cheeks sported a five o'clock shadow, giving him a slightly wolfish look.

She'd always had *such* a thing for dark, rakish-looking men.

And lordy, the man had the most glorious mouth she'd ever seen. Particularly now, with his eminently kissable lips lifted slightly at the corners as he offered her a tentative smile. The full frontal onslaught of his complete smile could probably rock the ground on which she stood.

"I really didn't mean to frighten you. Forgive me?"

She'd forgive him anything. Absolutely anything.

Even if he pulls out a chainsaw and a few various and sundry body parts? Get a grip, Gwen. Get out of here now.

That was her inner turtle speaking. She quickly told it to shut up. "The kitchen is one of the private areas of the house."

His eyes twinkled as he gave her a conspiratorial grin. "Don't tell on me. You keep my secret and I'll keep yours."

Her first instinct was confusion, then panic set in. Gwen kept only one secret—Hildy's history. But he couldn't know that. No one did. He had to be bluffing.

She tilted her head and eyed him with every bit of false bravado she could manage. "Why do you think I have a secret?"

He practically tsked. "Everyone has secrets. Besides, I'm an expert," he whispered, stepping even closer until he was only a foot away. So close she felt his warmth radiating toward her.

She almost swayed toward him, almost let that warmth envelop her more fully. "An expert?" She kept her feet planted, even as some deep, feminine part of her ached to step closer.

He nodded. "Absolutely. And I know one secret of yours. I don't imagine many people know you visit the kitchen dressed so...interestingly...late at night." His dark eyes grew darker. His jaw grew tight, and she heard the faint, ragged rasp of his breath.

Gwen followed his pointed stare, looking down at her body, clad in the silkiest, softest white nightgown she possessed. Then she swallowed. Hard. Seeing herself as he must be seeing her.

The deeply slashed neckline glittered with tiny pearl-like beads that picked up and reflected the meager light in the room. The fabric clung across her breasts, which were pushed high, plumped up and spilling over because of the tight bodice.

She could have claimed it was the cold autumn night that made her nipples pucker so tightly against the gown.

She could also have claimed to be engaged to Ben Affleck and having an affair with Brad Pitt. That didn't make it true.

Though she thought of how foolish she'd been not to grab her robe, a deep-rooted part of Gwen liked the admiration in his eyes. Her track record with romance was damned pathetic. The blow to her confidence brought on by her broken engagement had killed her instinct to even try to attract the opposite sex.

How funny. She now remembered what she'd once so very much *liked* about attracting the opposite sex. That look in a man's eye. The one that promised more than any words could. And hinted he could back up his unspoken promise anytime, anywhere.

Maybe even here and now.

"I didn't remember to bring my robe," she finally said, wondering how a perfect stranger could bring out the woman she'd thought was lost forever. "I should get it."

"Don't go to any trouble on my account." The intensity in his voice made the words less playful than he may have intended.

Watching his jaw clench, she sucked in a quick gulp of heady night air. How amazing that a man's stare could make her heart trip over itself as it beat restlessly within her chest. But not with fear. This was pure, one hundred percent excitement.

Gwen smoothed her hand against her nightie, nervously fingering the material. Its slickness slid between her fingers. The gown fit tightly to her hips, then fell in undulating waves to the floor. Two slits made the fabric gap from ankle to thigh. With every shift, another bit of skin would be revealed. Tempting. Tantalizing. Heightening the anticipation as any self-respecting wedding night negligee should.

Fate. Fate or one of the ghosts in this house had made the pipe in her room break right over most of her clothes, damaging all her nightgowns except this one...the one she was supposed to have worn on her honeymoon. The one she'd kept after she'd canceled the wedding, sold her dress, hocked her ring and delivered the cake to a homeless shelter.

Because, after finding her bastard of an ex giving more than dictation to his secretary a few days before their wedding, she'd needed one sultry, seductive, feminine thing, to remind her she was a desirable woman. His cheating had made her doubt herself. The nightie gave her confidence, though no one had ever seen her in it. Until now. And judging by the raw want in his eyes, this stranger definitely thought she was a desirable woman.

How amazing. How exciting. How...enticing.

Still, she wasn't stupid. This was risky business. She didn't know who this man with the hungry eyes was.

He seemed to sense her sudden misgivings because he stepped to the side, turning slightly away. He was now far enough that she didn't feel his warm breath on her skin. She shivered, wondering how she could miss the warmth of the stranger when by all rights she should be running like mad to her room.

"I really am sorry for frightening you."

"It's okay." Her voice sounded weak, breathy and nervous. She cleared her throat, then realized she meant it. "It's fine. I wasn't afraid. Not really."

She should have been, she knew that. She was alone in her nightgown, late at night, in a dark, quiet house, with a stranger. The normal reaction *should* have been fear. But for some reason his height didn't intimidate her. His breadth didn't, either, though his chest looked broad enough to tap-dance on. No doubt, this man, clad in skintight black fabric from his neck to his shoes, should have caused concern.

Maybe because she'd been burying the sensual part of herself for so long, Gwen had reacted with instant, unrelenting attraction. The kind that could turn stronger women than she into complete fools.

"What are you thinking?"

"That finding dark, handsome strangers in the kitchen late at night just doesn't happen to women like me."

He didn't laugh, or even smile, at her frankness. "And I don't often stumble across stunning blondes in nighties when I visit country inns. Or are you, perhaps, the ghost of this inn?"

"I'm entirely real." Then she paused. It was, after all, Halloween. The whole town believed she lived in a haunted house. She'd grown accustomed to strange happenings that had given her more than one sleepless night in recent months. And there were her aunt's spectral friends to consider. "Are *you* a ghost?"

This time, he did smile, his teeth glittering brilliantly white in the half darkness, making her heart trip again. Maybe her question hadn't been so ridiculous. No man this seductive could just stumble across her path. Not with her luck when it came to men.

"Not a ghost. I'm very real." He stepped closer again, until the tips of his shoes almost touched her toes. His pants brushed her gown; she could almost feel his leg against hers.

She didn't move away, even as the word *dangerous* flashed through her mind.

"Want me to prove it?"

Before she could answer—and Gwen couldn't say what her answer would have been—she felt the man grasp her fingers. He lifted them until she was almost touching his face. Then he pressed her fingers against his cheek. "Aren't ghosts cold?"

She nodded weakly, gauging the rough warmth of his skin, wondering if he'd read her mind when she'd thought earlier about how sexy his five o'clock shadow looked. "You're not cold."

Not cold. Hot. Magnetic. Seductive. Her fingertips scraped across the roughness of his cheek in a helpless, subtle caress.

"And spirits don't breathe, do they?"

Without warning, he moved her hand until her fingers brushed his lips. God, those lips. The other part of his face she'd found so arousing. Gwen's knees grew weak and shaky. She grabbed the counter with her free hand, then focused on the soft breath touching her fingertips as he slowly exhaled.

"Ghosts are also transparent," he continued, his voice so quiet, she almost had to strain to hear him. "I would say I'm pretty solid."

She knew what he meant. But he didn't come closer to let her feel just how solid he was. He was letting her decide. So she did. Not making a conscious decision to do so, she moved her feet forward, until her legs nearly cupped one of his.

Definitely solid. Hard. Thick and hot between her thighs. She wobbled on her bare feet and let out a long, shuddery sigh.

Oh, he was much more dangerous than any ghost. And here she was, reacting like every stupid bimbo in every scary movie ever made. Not running for the door when the killer's clanging around in the attic, but heading up the stairs toward the danger instead.

She scooted her feet apart, rubbing her calf against his pants...taking another step closer to the danger in the attic.

"See? I'm not a ghost." He turned her hand, staring at her wrist. Then, slowly, he drew it to his mouth and brushed his lips over the pulse point. She couldn't say for sure, but she thought she felt the tiniest flick of his tongue on her skin. Or else she imagined it, because she wanted to have felt it.

She moaned. No, he was not a ghost. But oh, heavens, with his breath caressing the tender skin of her wrist, she suddenly understood the seductive appeal in all those vampire novels.

"You're obviously not a ghost, either," he whispered before lowering her hand to her side. "We're both flesh and blood."

Once he'd let her go, Gwen took a tiny, physical step backward. And tried to take a great big mental one.

The stranger seemed to realize what he'd done...kissing the wrist of a stranger with the kind of sensual awareness Gwen had only ever read about in sultry novels. He met her stare, their eyes sharing knowledge of the boundaries they'd already crossed.

This was more dangerous than any supernatural threat. Because, at this moment, Gwen honestly didn't know if she'd make one sound of protest if he tried to take her in his arms.

To be completely honest, she doubted it.

JARED DIDN'T KNOW that he'd ever met a more desirable woman. Or, at least, not one he had ever desired more. She was curvy and feminine, made more so by the outrageously seductive nightgown she wore. Her hair was a mass of golden curls. It tangled around her face, tumbling over her shoulders, creating a peekaboo curtain over the high curves of her perfect breasts. She had eyes the color of his favorite brand of whiskey—golden brown, almost amber—and a delicate face with hints of strength in the cheekbones and determined little chin.

She was not petite, so he couldn't say why he found her delicate. Maybe it was the trembling of her lips, the hint of fear in her voice. But the fear couldn't hide the awareness between them from the moment they'd laid eyes on each other.

Who she was, he couldn't say. He'd never seen her before, so she probably wasn't from Derryville, unless she'd moved here recently. He planned to find out. Not just her character for this murder party. But her *real* identity. He had to know what kind of woman would get so into this weekend that she'd talk ghosts and play the frightened but seductive innocent.

"So, why are you here? In the kitchen, I mean? Were you looking for a snack?" She apparently wanted to normalize the conversation. Jared watched as she reached for the light switch on the wall and flipped it up. But nothing happened, no overhead fixture brightened the shadowy room. "Must have blown a bulb."

Undeterred, she stepped to another cabinet. She seemed familiar with the room, because she felt her way, pushing a switch and turning on a small lamp beside a wall phone. When added to the stove light and the illumination from the hall, the room no longer seemed as dim and mysterious.

Better able to see, he was unable to resist casting another leisurely glance at her, studying her long, wildly curling hair, her bare throat and her shoulders covered only by the tiny spaghetti straps of her nightgown. Then lower. He found himself almost wishing she hadn't turned on the extra light. Because now, there was no way to disguise his instant male reaction.

He watched her twist her own fingers together, then smooth them over her gown, clenching the fabric. He knew she was resisting the urge to pull her hands up to cover her breasts. She didn't want him to see her awareness.

Impossible. He didn't know her name, but he knew a whole lot about her, just the same. She was beautiful. She was intoxicating. She was exciting. She wanted him.

Really, what more did a man need to know?

Besides, she wasn't indecent, not at all. Her nightgown was thin, but not transparent. He'd seen plenty of women in dresses that covered less. So, no, it wasn't her apparel that made the situation so damned provocative.

It was the heat in what should have been a cold room. The awareness between two strangers. The purely physical reaction that made it tough to think, tough to breathe. Neither of them was doing a good job at hiding that physical reaction. Her, with the goose bumps on her exposed skin, the pointed tips of her nipples against her silk gown making his mouth water. Him, wondering if he was going to burst the seam of his pants.

"Don't tell me," he finally said, respecting her unspoken wish to slow things down. "You're a movie star, stopping at the inn on the way to your next film location."

He earned a slight laugh. "Not by a long shot. Though, we do have a couple of old-time movie stars staying with us this weekend. At least, that's who they say they are."

He nodded, not surprised. The cast of characters widened...how creative of Mick to bring Hollywood into the mystery. Putting his curiosity about the other players in this game aside, he continued to speculate on this particular one. "So, are you a bride on her wedding night, with a jealous husband about to burst through that door?"

She shook her head.

"A woman being gaslighted by some wicked man and a maid?"

"Uh-uh."

He thought about it, wondering what other possible scenarios his cousin might have come up with for his cast of characters. "Please tell me you're not a Rapunzel type who's eventually going to need rescuing from a high tower. Because heights and I don't like each other very much."

She laughed softly. "I'm just a simple innkeeper."

"Ahh." He reached out and touched her hair, picking up one long, curly gold tendril. Then he smiled, thinking of one of his favorite Charlie Brown movies from his childhood. "Do innkeeper's wives have naturally curly hair?"

She didn't react to the joke, didn't even seem to have heard him. Her eyelids fluttered, then closed.

God, this was getting intense again. He dropped his hand.

When she opened her eyes, instead of answering his teasing question, she focused on the *wife* part. "I'm not married."

"Me neither. Not even involved."

She murmured something that sounded like *good.*

"So, what's your name? Why are you here?" she asked.

"The name's easy." He almost gave himself away by laughing as he attempted a James Bond accent. Connery, of course—the classic Bond. Moore had been a caricature, Brosnan was merely okay. And he couldn't even remember the name of that other guy. "The name is Stone. Miles Stone."

She didn't even seem to notice the hideously bad joke his cousin had foisted on him with the name: milestone.

"I'm Gwen Compton."

He gave her a half smile. "Nice to meet you, Gwen."

Her lips curled up at the corners and her amber eyes twinkled in the muted light. "It's nice to be met."

Though Jared Winchester—the private, introspective author—would probably have then propelled the conversation along more normal lines, he decided to keep playing the game. He'd use this mystery scenario to be more outrageous, more provocative than he might normally be with a woman he'd just met.

Miles Stone answered, not Jared Winchester. "As for the second part of your question…what am I doing here?"

He stepped close again, until he felt her calf brushing against his pants. She licked her lips, but didn't step away.

"Yes?"

He reached up and touched her throat, sliding his finger up to caress her earlobe as he leaned closer, until their mouths were a breath apart. Then he filled that miniscule space with a whisper. "I'm afraid if I told you that, I'd have to kill you."

3

IF I TOLD YOU THAT I'd have to kiss you.

Only, he hadn't said kiss, had he? No, surely he'd said kill. But Gwen didn't care. Kiss was what flashed in her mind. Kiss was what echoed in her brain, tempting her to be outrageous. A kiss might be daring enough to test that sexiness, that womanliness, that had eluded her since her failed engagement.

So, kiss she did. When the possible ax murderer who'd just threatened her life leaned close until their breaths mingled, she grabbed his face and proceeded to kiss the lips off him.

Of course, she'd known he was joking with the killing part. In spite of the aura of danger, she'd felt sure from the moment they'd started speaking that he was no threat to her. At least not physically. Mentally? Well, in that respect, she wasn't so sure. Her libido had been on high alert all night. An unusual occurrence for a woman who hadn't had sex in over a year.

But she was entitled. She hadn't done a single daring thing today. Besides, it wasn't like she was getting engaged to a cheating bastard—*again.* She was just stealing a kiss. One kiss.

Twining her fingers in his hair, she tugged him closer until their lips could meet fully. He tasted dangerous and delicious. She didn't get too serious, just slid her lips against his, letting them part the tiniest bit, but no further. His body was close, a thin aura of awareness the only thing separating them. He made no effort to pull her tighter, letting her take what she wanted.

So she took. Without thought, without common sense, with only a bit of Halloween-and-moonlight-inspired madness.

Finally, after what could have been five seconds or five minutes, she pulled her mouth away. She felt no embarrassment. She'd kissed a stranger. Not a big deal in the scheme of things, right? She hadn't robbed a bank, or fled from the police or been around during a shootout. Unlike some members of her family.

"Okay," she said with a soft sigh.

"Okay?" he asked, looking surprised—but not displeased.

"Yes. That was my one impulsive act for the day."

"That was it, huh?"

She nodded. "Yep. One a day's my quota."

He frowned. "Too bad." Reaching up, he traced the line of her jaw with the tip of his finger. "But, you know, it's only an hour until midnight. Wanna stick around and see what impulse you feel like giving into tomorrow?"

Naughty. Very naughty. She liked that about him. "I'm afraid I've gotten it out of my system. One kiss was all I needed."

"That's like saying all you need is one piece of rich, decadent chocolate." His voice thickened. "Some things just *scream* to be tried again."

She nibbled her lip. He was right. With some things, one was never enough. And this man's kisses could be more addictive than chocolate. "I've done enough trying for one night. At least now, if you end up killing me, I'll die after having enjoyed a nice kiss."

He tsked. "I only kill bad guys."

Though she suspected he was teasing, his voice sounded somewhat serious. "I'm not a bad guy."

"No, you're the mysterious, sultry, kissable innkeeper whose story I don't yet know." He spoke so strangely, playfully almost, fitting in with the surreal mood she'd felt all night.

"I don't have a story."

He brushed a long tendril of hair off her face, his fingertips lingering on her temple. "Everyone has a story."

"What's yours?" She clarified. "Or, at least, what of yours can you tell me without needing to do me in?"

He laughed softly, and her breath hitched at the low, resonant sound. She liked the way this man sounded as much as she liked the way he looked.

"Maybe I don't have a story, either."

"You have 'story' written all over you."

"Too bad it's not in braille," he said, all flirtatious charm. A twinkle in his eye dared her to follow his meaning.

She did...and chuckled. "Okay, Mr. Stone, you're very entertaining, but I do like to know something about the men I stumble over in darkened kitchens and kiss against their will."

"Who said it was against my will?"

"You certainly didn't ask for it," she pointed out.

"I didn't ask the cheerleading squad at my high school to flash me and my buddies, either." He grinned. "Some things you want are just obvious."

"Like that second piece of chocolate," she admitted, conceding the point. Then a gentle warmth spread through her as she focused on the *want* part of his statement. He wanted her. Or he'd at least wanted her kiss. So, she wasn't the only one affected by the seductive atmosphere in the air tonight.

Trying to turn this strange encounter into something more normal, she stepped away from him and walked to the huge storage freezer. Opening it, she pulled out a tray of frozen pumpkin muffins. After she'd set it on the counter, she glanced over her shoulder, aware that he watched every move she made.

"Breakfast?"

She nodded. "You are staying the entire weekend?"

"Yes."

She wondered if he could tell she was pleased. Then she sighed. "We've got a full house. It's going to be busy. I'm sure I'll be dead tired by Sunday night."

He laughed, as if she'd made a joke. "Right. *Dead* tired. I probably will be, too." Though she raised an inquiring brow, he didn't elaborate. "So, who else is here for this holiday weekend? Just who is sleeping in this house tonight, other than the innkeeper, the ex-movie stars...and me?"

She nibbled her lip as she thought about it, trying to remember everyone who'd checked in. So many faces—some familiar, but some having come into Derryville for only this one event. A weekend magazine mention of the new haunted inn had appeared in a Chicago paper in time to get them several last-minute reservations. People appeared willing to travel a long way to spend a night in a haunted house on October 31. A spooky B & B was perfect for grown-ups who wanted to give in to their deep-rooted need to revisit childhood and scare themselves silly on Halloween. Without giving up pampering and comfort, of course.

"Well, in addition to the older couple, there's a pretty young doctor," she said, remembering the woman she'd shown to the Lady in Red room. "Someone who says he's an archeologist, and one woman who works at a museum.

An older man with a thick foreign accent and a psychic from New Orleans. A couple of local residents. My aunt checked the rest of them in."

They'd been busy getting everyone settled, plus hosting their spooky cocktail hour in the front parlor, for which everyone had dressed in costumes. She hadn't had time to question Hildy about who the other guests were. She'd said her hellos, chatting briefly with the Derryville residents who'd come for their grand opening. After serving drinks and hors d'oeuvres, she'd gone to change into her own costume for the trick-or-treaters.

He seemed amused. "So, we have a couple of movie stars, a doctor, a mysterious foreigner, a professor type and a psychic?"

"And the ghosts, of course," she added, wondering if her tone had made it sound like she'd thought the foreign-sounding man was mysterious. Because, truthfully, that was what she'd thought when she'd met the man, who was probably sleeping peacefully on the third floor. But she'd hate to think her personal reactions to her guests were so easily discerned.

"Oh, yes, of course, mustn't forget the ghosts." He obviously thought she was joking.

She could have explained, but how could one explain the unexplainable? Hildy did a much better job of that, anyway. Mr. Stone would likely get an earful about the ghosts at some point; she didn't want to spoil the mood now by getting into details about spooks. He probably already thought she was crazy for kissing him. He didn't need any more evidence that he'd landed in the *Twilight Zone* here at the Little Bohemie Inn.

"So," he said, "I guess you'll claim this is your average, everyday collection of guests at an inn?"

She countered with a pointed stare. "No less average than your everyday assassin."

"I'm not an assassin."

"Hit man?"

He rolled his eyes. "Please."

She waited, raising an expectant brow.

"All right, I'll tell you what I can. But you can't mention this to anyone unless you trust them implicitly. No one can know I'm here yet." He lowered his voice. "It could be dangerous."

Dangerous. Oh, yes, definitely. "Tell me at least one thing. Are you running *from* something or *to* something?"

He thought about it for a moment. "I'm not running. But I am *pursuing*." He gave her a look of startling intensity, loading his comment with double meaning.

Pursuing. Hmm. A hot romance? A weekend tryst? Mindless, erotic sex with a complete stranger?

"Go on," she prodded, her voice sounding breathy.

He leaned across the counter, resting his elbows on its surface. Meeting her eyes, as if willing her to believe him, he said, "I'm undercover, Gwen. Deep, deep undercover."

She lifted a brow. "You're a cop?"

"It's a bit more complicated than that."

When he didn't continue, she speculated aloud. Lifting her hand, she ticked off her fingers one at a time. "Deep undercover, on a mission, deadly if provoked, not a cop, a hit man or an assassin." Giving him a cheeky grin, she concluded, "Hmm...you must be a woman armed with a high-limit credit card, scouting out Sak's the night before their annual one-day sale."

Not waiting for his response, she walked around from behind the counter and pulled out a chair at the massive, butcher block kitchen table. She sat down, even as the tiny voice in her brain urged her to go up to her temporary room and go back to bed.

Alone. Now.

But even as that voice of caution whispered, she knew she'd ignore it. Tonight was becoming too exciting to consider leaving. The thrill was intoxicating. The danger appealed to a part of Gwen she thought she'd lost forever. She somehow found herself feeling like the wild, uninhibited girl she'd once been, before tragedy and sadness had made her decide—if only in her subconscious—to play it safe and careful, to subdue the wild part of herself that had so often led her into trouble.

The floor was cold against her bare toes, so she lifted her feet, resting them on the bottom rung of the chair. Her white nightgown did an adequate job of covering her hips and thighs, but she kept her hands in her lap, holding everything in place.

But the gown was pulled tighter in this position. Sure, her legs were covered, but they were also outlined by the silky fabric. Her thighs were clearly delineated, as was the slight gap between them. She squeezed them together, watching him notice as he took the chair next to hers.

"That was a good guess," he finally said, his voice thin.

Good guess. What guess? She suddenly could barely remember her own name, much less what on earth they'd been talking about.

"But I don't think I'd be tempted to kill someone for buying the pair of shoes I wanted."

Ahh. Now she remembered. "Have you ever *seen* the discounts at Sak's one-day sale?"

He shook his head.

"You might be tempted. Particularly if they're *great* shoes and the person who's buying them looks like one of

Cinderella's stepsisters, jamming a too-tubby foot in because they're cheap."

"Possibly, but there are two things wrong with your theory."

He leaned closer, until his knees almost touched hers, and her hair ruffled with his softly exhaled breaths. God, the man was seductive. Even talking about ridiculous things like hit men and shoe sales, all her nerve endings were at the highest state of alert. No amber here, she was full on red and waiting to see what sensual weapons he had left in his arsenal.

Though she knew she should have left, she didn't regret staying. She wanted to know what would happen next. What he'd say. What he'd do. And how she'd react to it.

"What two things?" she finally managed to ask, trying to keep a coherent thought in her head. Difficult when she was so distracted by the way his skin smelled, like salty sea air, and the way his breath brought goose bumps to her bare throat.

"First, from what I know of Derryville, I don't imagine there's a Sak's within a hundred miles."

True. Coming here last winter had been definite culture shock. But small-town life had grown on her. "Point taken."

"And second, I don't use my dangerous weapons against anyone but the really bad people. Not greedy shoppers with fat feet, no matter how annoying they might be."

"For the record I'm not one of those greedy shoppers."

As if he couldn't help himself, he leaned closer. She had no idea what he was doing until he touched one of her feet, lifting it off the rung and cupping it in his big, warm hand.

Gwen wasn't a petite woman, but she thought she did have rather nice, slender feet. Feet which had suddenly become massive erogenous zones, because she ached to feel his fingers higher on her body. Much higher. Between her legs. On her breasts. At her throat. Against her cheek. Everywhere she wanted to be touched by him.

"And you don't have fat feet," he said, continuing to stroke her foot, as if wanting to warm her sensitized skin. His touch ignited a flood of sensation that increased the temperature throughout her body. She was left wondering why no man had ever found that incredibly sensitive area…right *there.* Yes, that spot high on the inside of her foot, near her ankle. The one that almost made her squirm because, though the touch was focused in one location, she was feeling it everywhere.

She couldn't help emitting a tiny moan. God, if the man's hands on her foot could make her shift in her seat, because of her body's damp reaction, how on earth would she handle it if he ever touched *elsewhere?*

Finally, as if realizing he was erotically touching the foot of a near stranger, he let her go, gently lowering her leg until she rested her heel back on the chair rung.

When she'd started breathing again, a day or two…minute or two…*whatever*…later, she cleared her throat. Sitting here, being so affected by him, she needed to know more about the man. "Just who do you use your dangerous weapons on, Miles?"

He paused, looking like he was trying to decide how to answer. She recognized the naughty setup she'd provided, and wondered if her subconscious had done it on purpose. Probably. Because she'd certainly been thinking about one of Mr. Stone's "weapons" in particular, and who she'd like him to use it on.

Uh, yeah, *that* one. And oh, right, *her.*

Finally, seeming to decide not to make a sultry comeback in spite of the opening, he frowned. "Can I trust you?"

She nodded. "Even though I grabbed you and kissed you in a moment of Halloween-induced insanity, yes, you can trust me."

He tsked, as if reminding her that they'd already had that argument. Then, reaching into an inside pocket of his black leather jacket—a well-worn, shoulder-hugging kind of jacket—he pulled out a photo identification card. And a badge.

"You *are* a cop?"

He shook his head and pointed to a logo. She made out some words, but didn't recognize them. "The Shop? What's that?"

"You've heard of the FBI, the CIA, the Secret Service, the Department of Homeland Security?"

"Sure."

"We're the deepest, darkest subunit of every one of them."

She raised a brow. "You're a secret agent?"

His nod was grave. "Yes."

Gwen's first thought was that, in spite of his very looks and smooth delivery, Miles wasn't a very *good* secret agent. Secret agents didn't go around telling people they were secret agents on undercover missions, did they? Except, maybe, for Austin Powers. Or James Bond when he wanted to get laid.

Whoa. That mental image distracted her for a good twenty seconds. She was no Bond girl, but the thought was enticing. Gwen Compton didn't have quite the ring of Pussy Galore or Alotta Fagina, but she was at least dressed for the part. Her hair—normally flat and straight—did look extremely fabulous tonight, due to the leftover Glenda the

Good Witch curls. And she'd kissed him like some bold, confident mystery woman. Not to mention they'd met under rather unusual circumstances. In a dark kitchen. On the spookiest night of the year. When she was half-naked.

Well, no wonder he'd started to act like James Bond!

"I wouldn't have told you this," he continued, "but I need your help. I need an ally inside this house." Reaching down, he picked up a dark briefcase. She hadn't even noticed it.

While she watched silently, he opened the case. She glimpsed a manila envelope, in which appeared to be a number of papers and photos, with notations in a foreign language. The case also contained some sort of radio and electronic devices.

Miles pulled out a photograph, placed it on the tabletop, and pushed it toward her with the tip of one finger. "Boris Rockinova. Ex-KGB agent turned international arms dealer."

Gwen stared at the picture, a black-and-white 8 x 10 of a middle-aged, balding man. Normal-looking. He could have bagged her groceries or sold her a car and she'd never have given him a second look. She raised a doubtful brow. "*He's* a terrorist type?"

Miles nodded, retaining his serious expression.

"And you think he might be here? In Derryville?" She heard the skepticism in her own voice.

"I think he might be right here...in this *house.* Our contacts say he's set up a meeting here this weekend with potential buyers, including a high-level member of an organized crime group from New York. We don't have the identity, but we know he's working with a woman. This woman, code name Miss Jones, is supposed to make contact with him to arrange a weapons buy in preparation for a crime planned for the port of New York."

"Who is she?"

"Not sure." He glanced down at her body. "But I know she's not you. The communication we intercepted says the woman will identify herself to our suspect by her code name, Miss Jones, and will reveal a star-shaped birthmark on her right collarbone."

She followed his stare toward her own low neckline and grinned. "Good thing I'm not wearing a turtleneck."

He nodded, not cracking a smile, still intense and secretive, focused on his mission. "A very good thing."

The heat in his stare told her he wasn't merely talking about any phantom birthmark. She swallowed hard, trying to focus on their conversation, not the attraction still snapping between them. "How can you know all this?"

"We know a lot about the people in this inn this weekend," he admitted. "That elderly couple?"

She raised an inquiring brow.

"Counterfeiters."

Her jaw dropped.

"Double-check any money they give you."

"They paid with a credit card," she murmured, still not fully able to wrap her mind around this whole crazy scenario.

Maybe this guy was loco, maybe he was playing games with her, perhaps he was even an escapee from a mental institution. Maybe he was playing a big fat Halloween prank. Her instincts said there was more to this story than he'd said, that his charm hid as much as it revealed. Conventional wisdom told her she should be on the phone, out the door or arming herself with something sharp. That's certainly what any quiet turtle would do.

To hell with that.

She forced the thought away. Gwen wasn't stupid enough to react foolishly out of a need to do something reckless and exciting for a change. But something about his story rang true, though she suspected he hadn't told her everything. Perhaps he was telling her only as much of the truth as he could.

He had identification, a briefcase full of documents and, if she wasn't mistaken, what looked like surveillance equipment. He was also intense and charming, suave and smooth-talking. Obviously intelligent, adept at slipping in the shadows.

The CIA, or the Shop, or whatever it was, could do worse. So it wasn't entirely impossible. And if there was any chance, whatsoever, that Miles was indeed who he said he was, she might have a dangerous criminal sleeping under her roof.

An international arms dealer, along with the ghosts, was enough to ruin any fledgling inn. At least for the 51.5 weeks of the year not involving Halloween. And that didn't even take into account the whole "being murdered in her bed" scenario.

"All right," she finally said. Her voice sounded both a little skeptical and a little afraid. "I'll help you, Mr. Stone. I'll be your ally this weekend. Tell me what you want me to do."

4

JARED WASN'T SURE how she managed to capture that perfect tone, a mixture of excitement, doubt and even a hint of genuine fear ringing so clearly in her voice. She had the "frightened blonde late at night alone in a spooky house" role down pat.

Not to mention she was beautiful. Charming. Funny. With a lyrical whisper and an intoxicating laugh.

And, God, she smelled good. Like apples and cinnamon. Warm and spicy. She brought to mind every single one of his favorite scents, heightening sensation and evoking long-buried memories and emotions. He could breathe deeply and almost taste autumn.

He'd never known how much he'd miss that until he'd moved away from here. Chicago was a city with no orchards, no pumpkin patches. No rich aroma of dew-soaked fallen leaves on a crisp October day, punctuated by a whiff of someone's first fire of the season, or a hot-cider stand along the road.

Being with Gwen had brought all those sense memories rushing to his mind. For that alone he'd have liked her.

"What can I do to help?" she prompted.

"You've already been helpful. Filling me in on the guests, letting me know who I might be up against is beneficial."

Who he might be up against...a loaded way to put it. He wondered if she noticed the way he suddenly had to shift in his seat at the image of who he'd very much *like* to be up against.

Her. Against the counter. Against the refrigerator. On the table. Hot and frantic. Then slow and erotic. "Do you mind if I get some water?" he asked, definitely needing to cool down.

She immediately stood.

"I can help myself."

"It's no bother." Her voice shook. So did her legs. She wobbled as she walked. Obviously he wasn't the only one who'd had a visual image of being "up against" someone.

This weekend was shaping up as one that would long live in his memories. All because of the intriguing innkeeper. Certainly not because of his cousin's party, which seemed to be off to a slow start if everyone else in the house was already asleep.

When she returned with a bottle of springwater, he used the shock of the cold container against his fingertips to regain his mental focus. He saw her cast another curious glance toward his open briefcase. While he didn't fear she was fluent in Russian and able to read the documents on the Glanovsky case, he didn't want her seeing any of the more graphic photos. He picked up the file and slid it beneath everything else. Then he put his badge and fake ID into the briefcase, too. "Sorry. Top secret."

"More of that, 'knowledge is death' stuff?"

He heard a slight chuckle in her voice. "Yes."

"Okay. But you still haven't told me what I can do to help. I'd like to get this situation resolved soon." A worried expression tugged at her brow. "You don't suppose this...arms dealer guy has any explosives here in the house, do you?"

He shrugged. "It's possible."

"Oh, great. I'd really rather not wake up tomorrow dead, having been blown up to heaven because some terrorist can't keep his stick of dynamite from shooting off prematurely."

Instantly understanding the double entendre, he couldn't contain a low laugh. He enjoyed this woman's quick, naughty wit.

She blushed. So, maybe she hadn't intended to sound so damned provocative. Either way, she was absolutely beguiling.

Who she was, and how she knew his cousin Mick, were things he'd have to find out soon. He hoped like hell she wasn't his playboy cousin's latest conquest, because he didn't know that even family loyalty would keep him from stealing her away.

Jared had always filled the role of big brother to Mick. They were different, in looks and personality. But there'd been a bond between them from childhood. They'd been more like brothers than cousins, particularly since they'd each had only sisters.

Jared had covered Mick's back more than once when his cousin had gotten himself into trouble with his smart-ass attitude. Hell, he still had a half moon-shaped scar on his left hand from saving Mick's hide back in high school. That particular time, one of the girls his cousin had jilted had thrown a high-heeled shoe at Mick's head. Jared had intercepted and its heel had left the scar.

When they were kids, he'd never taken advantage of being a year older to pick on his cousin, abandon him in the woods, cheat to win at Atari, or steal his Matchbox cars.

Gwen, however, was no Matchbox car. If she was Mick's date.... *No.* She couldn't be. Mick liked giggly, bouncy cheerleader types with big smiles and bigger hair. Not a seductress who could devastate with a flash of wit. Gwen wasn't Mick's type. Besides, even if she were, he knew his cousin well enough to know he wouldn't let this woman roam around without him in a sexy white nightie.

Not Mick's date. No way.

Judging by the absence of a ring on her left hand—along with no tan line to indicate she usually wore one there—he figured she was technically single. Damn good thing. Because he sensed their weekend was going to be downright combustible.

"All right," he said, finally responding to her offer to help. "You can do something. You can start by telling me if the man in this photo could be here at the inn." When she started to shake her head, he frowned. "Remember, he could be in disguise. For instance, the man with the foreign accent, the one you checked in today. Does he look like this guy?"

She nibbled at her fingertip, scrunching her brow in concentration. Jared liked watching her play along as if she truly believed she might help catch a criminal. In reality, if he'd stepped in here claiming to be a superspy, she'd probably be reaching for the phone to call for the men in the white coats.

"The man who checked in today was a little thinner." Her eyes widened. "But, you know, if he were wearing a toupee, and glasses, and some kind of body girdle, it could be him."

Body girdle. He nearly snorted. From Gwen's description of the man, he'd first thought it was Mick's father, Uncle Frankie, who was using a fake accent. Uncle Frankie did a fair impression of the Godfather. Particularly after he'd downed a few beers—or whenever Sophie, Mick's sister, had brought a boyfriend around as a teenager.

But the day that man would wear a body girdle was the day Jared would willingly sit through an ice-dancing competition. *Never*. So, either Uncle Frankie was *not* the foreign-sounding gentleman. Or else Aunt Marnie had finally nagged him into giving up those all-you-can-eat fried chicken specials.

"All right, so it's possible he's here," Jared said, trying to remain serious and in character as he pictured his Uncle Frankie eating yogurt, or anything steamed.

"What do we do? Should we call someone?"

"I *am* someone. Remember?"

She frowned. "But you're alone."

"I have you," he reminded her, smiling in a way that probably hinted at just how much he'd *like* to have her.

"I suppose...but are you sure you don't need backup? I mean, do you know anyone else here in town you can call on?"

Yeah, actually. He knew a lot of people here in Derryville, from his kindergarten teacher to the owner of the feed store. From the girls who worked in the hair salon on Great Lakes Lane to most of the men on the small police force. He'd been away for ten years. Not long enough for things to change in a town like Derryville. That was one of the reasons he'd had to escape, to break free. Growing up here had been like living in a fish tank. Everyone saw every move, commented on every turn.

Getting out hadn't been something he'd wanted to do. It had been what he'd *had* to do. If for no other reason than to get some damn privacy for the first time in his life.

Still, during the few times he'd come back, he had felt a twinge or two of nostalgia. No matter how much he'd longed to escape Derryville, it would always be home to him. Particularly now. In the fall. Yes, summer had become his favorite season since moving to Chicago. But sitting here, with a woman who smelled of apples and had golden eyes and hair the color of sunshine, he remembered that it hadn't always been that way.

As a kid, nothing had compared to the excitement he'd felt when October rolled around. His thoughts would turn to scary costumes, pranks and parties. Many of his favorite childhood memories were from the holidays from October to December.

Maybe that's why coming home was feeling so right tonight. On Halloween.

"Miles?"

He finally answered her nearly forgotten question. "Yeah. I have people I can call on who are nearby. If the need arises."

Like family. His cousin Mick, and Mick's sister Sophie. Their parents. Jared's own parents were snowbirds who'd already taken off to spend Halloween with his sister and her kids in Florida. But his grandfather was still here. And everyone in Derryville knew his grandfather, Samuel Winchester. He'd been police chief for twenty years before stepping aside so his son, Jared's dad, could take over the job.

Then he'd waited, expecting Jared to do the same. Everyone expected that, knowing Mick was too much of a playboy to be a cop. When Jared hadn't... Well, his grandfather was from the old school. Betraying tradition meant betraying your family. He and his grandfather hadn't had a real conversation in eight years.

"Why are you frowning?"

Jared thrust the disturbing thoughts of his grandfather out of his mind and focused instead on his attractive playmate in this weekend's game. "It's nothing."

"So, do you have a plan, or backup, or anything?"

"I can take care of myself." Reaching into his pocket, he pulled out the small, fake handgun, which would be useful only if she pulled out a cigar and asked for a light. Her eyes widened, so he slid it back into his pocket, patting the bulge in the leather jacket. "As you can see, I came prepared. We'll be fine."

She pursed her bottom lip. "I don't particularly care for guns. But my Aunt Hildy knows how to handle one."

Aunt Hildy. Another player? "Is she here this weekend?"

"Oh, of course." Then she frowned. "We have to keep her in the dark about this. Aunt Hildy is a trifle...eccentric. If she had the faintest idea what was going on, she'd want to start snooping in rooms or doing full body searches of the guests."

Jared briefly considered offering to help with the full body searches—at least of one particular guest. The one sitting beside him, looking so damn sexy he couldn't think straight.

"Okay, we won't tell her," he agreed.

"So, should we, uh, do anything right now?"

Oh, yeah, he could definitely think of some things he'd like to be doing right now. But he had the feeling she was talking about the game, not about hot and heavy sex. "I don't think so," he replied. "I could just use a little time to formulate a strategy."

"About what's going to happen this weekend?"

"Right." He smiled. "About what's going to happen in this house this weekend." *Hopefully, quite a lot.*

At some point, they'd have to get serious. No way was he leaving here without knowing her true identity, address and phone number. But for right now, at least, he was having far too much fun to drop the act.

And why shouldn't he have some fun? Do something different to break up the monotony, to make him feel in on the action, like he was a social being, after being exactly the opposite for so long?

Jared Winchester, the writer, was a reserved, introspective thinker. A loner. Self-reliant, self-sufficient. He worked alone, spending hours every day poring over case files, interviews and histories. He tried to get into the minds of people who'd committed some horrific crimes, and also to tap into the emotion and reactions felt by their victims.

He hadn't made much effort to socialize with others outside his circle in ages. His friends were people like him, with the same interests. Understandable, perhaps. But so very boring.

He almost didn't remember the kind of man he'd been before he'd become Jared Winchester, criminalist, former FBI profiler, true-crime novelist and internationally known serial-murder expert. He could hardly recall what it was like to be nothing but the oldest grandson of a respected family in a small, close-knit town. Nor why he'd run like hell away from here as soon as he was old enough to do so. Particularly now, when for the first time in ages he had such a strong sense of being in the right place, at the right time, for all the right reasons.

Maybe this weekend—during the craziest, wildest holiday season of the year—he'd have a chance to figure out what those reasons were. Perhaps, as Miles Stone, he could do exactly that.

Because Stone was a different type of man altogether. The secret agent was a dangerous, provocative daredevil. A thrill-seeker, a live-in-the-moment guy who'd face danger with as much enthusiasm as he'd face a beautiful blonde in a white negligee.

There really was no deciding. For the next few days, he would *be* Miles Stone. And maybe, in doing so, he could figure out just who the hell Jared Winchester was.

GWEN DIDN'T THINK she'd ever been as attracted to a man who, by all rights, should have scared the bejesus out of her. He didn't, though. After those first few minutes, she'd honestly felt very comfortable with this dark, handsome stranger.

Well, comfortable wasn't the right word, since she was alert, edgy and aware of every move he made, and of every answering quiver in her own body. But she wasn't afraid of him. She didn't itch to get away, to seek the safety of her own room. She wanted to stay, which surprised her. Since being so badly burned by Rick, her ex-fiancé, she hadn't trusted any man well enough to even engage him in conversation.

She snuck a surreptitious glance at the wall clock. Going on an hour now. Some kind of record. Another sixty minutes and it would be nearly midnight, the witching hour, on Halloween. She shivered lightly, but not with fear...with pure anticipation.

She couldn't remember the last time she'd felt so alive. Danger had always made her feel that way. She'd just made herself forget that when she'd decided to try to live a safe, conservative life.

"So tell me how you ended up here, Gwen. I want to know everything about you." His half smile took any nosiness out of his query. She wondered if he used the technique on suspects.

"I don't know that my history will be of any help to you."

"Let me be the judge of that. Have you been in the innkeeping business long?" he asked.

Ha. In the innkeeping business. She wondered what he'd say if she told him she used to be an executive V.P. with a nationally known hotel chain. That she'd once had an office on Beacon Street. That she'd had a staff of hundreds, made a bunch of money, socialized with the Boston elite and been engaged to one of the most sought-after bachelors in the northeast.

And that she'd been terribly unhappy.

Being engaged to one of the most sought-after bachelors in Boston had not been all it was cracked up to be. Particularly when that bastard...er...bachelor, was two things. One, a womanizer who was unable to keep his pants zipped. And two, an underhanded competitor who had been using Gwen to gain information about Gwen's company. Information he'd planned to use against Gwen's boss, a man she respected and admired.

Her relationship with Rick had definitely been enough to build a hard little shell around her heart. And reinforced her belief that safe is best. "The inn opened earlier this month. We hadn't expected to be able to open for business until the New Year, but managed to hurry things along to take advantage of Halloween."

"Convenient. Given old man Marsden's reputation, I'm sure Halloween weekend was the perfect time of year to open this inn."

She gulped. "You know about Mr. Marsden?"

He glanced down at her. "Of course, we've been investigating this area. Anyone as colorful as Nathaniel Marsden would turn up."

"Yes, colorful," she agreed, wondering if he knew exactly how "colorful" Nathaniel Marsden had been. Few did. Only those who'd known him in the old days knew the man had once been called Fat Lip Nathan. Not only because he'd had a prominent lower lip, but also because he'd frequently lost his temper and punched anyone who annoyed him back in his Chicago days.

Aunt Hildy had told her about him after the lawyer had tracked her aunt down and told her Nathaniel Marsden had willed his house in Derryville to his only love. His partner in crime. His teenage girlfriend, Hildy Compton. Who'd apparently had a thing for guys with big, gooshy lower lips in her youth.

"How do you like Derryville?"

She couldn't stop a wide smile. "It's different from Boston. Homier. Which is funny since my homes have always been in cities. I should be conditioned to think of home as a high-rise with a million people, nightmarish traffic and lots of shops nearby."

He raised a brow. "Doesn't exactly describe Derryville."

No, it didn't. Which made it strange that she felt so comfortable here, like she'd finally found the place she was meant to be. She'd felt that from the first time she'd seen this wonderfully wicked-looking old house, when she'd arrived last winter. With Hildy's help she'd been determined to make a fresh start, to rediscover herself and find the inner well of happiness and self-confidence Rick had so carelessly destroyed.

Funny, for the first time since she'd arrived, she began to think about the possibility of being here and not being alone. She found herself wondering if the CIA or the Office of Homeland Security, or this Shop place, had a deep, dark, secret office in Derryville.

One with permanent agents who stuck around for a while.

AS GWEN CONTINUED her fictional account of how she and her Aunt Hildy had put so much work into getting the inn ready to open, Jared glanced around the kitchen. He'd never been inside this house, so he couldn't say for sure, but there was a hint of fresh paint permeating the air. The place looked cleaner, brighter than he'd have expected for a long-vacant house.

The kitchen's condition gave him a moment's pause, but he shrugged off the unease. His cousin Mick had never done things halfway. Mick could easily have called in a few favors and gotten somebody to work on the house before the party.

After they'd talked for a while about the inn and the town, Gwen looked at the clock. "It's late. I should say good-night."

She stood, pushing her chair away with the backs of her knees. Certainly it wasn't by design that her legs were inches from his, that her waist and midriff were perfectly aligned with his appreciative stare. That with one small tilt of his head, he could savor a much closer glimpse of the deep vee of her neckline. The curves of her breasts held his attention, the long tangle of blond hair not concealing the dark tip of a taut nipple, so nicely outlined by the satiny white fabric.

"You're sure you want to...go?"

Say no.

"No."

He smiled.

"But I have to," she added.

Silently admitting defeat, Jared pushed his own chair back. He needed to track down Mick, anyway, to find out where he was supposed to be staying in this house of games.

He rose to his feet, his body brushing against hers as he made that long, sultry slide from seated to standing erect.

Very erect, if truth be told.

He didn't step back, remaining beside her. Close enough that they shared the same space, breathed the same warm air...and likely thought the same wicked thoughts.

"Good night, Gwen." Then, unable to resist, he cupped her cheek. "Don't worry. I won't let anything happen to you."

Before she could slip away, he answered his body's instinctive demand for one more taste, one more tiny sample of her lips. He lowered his mouth to hers, and this time heard her moan of acceptance as she parted her lips. Their tongues met, tangled in a slow, sultry dance of heat and pleasure that promised as much as it enticed. Aroused as much as it satisfied.

Jared found himself wondering if he'd made a tactical error. No way was he going to be able to let her go, to walk away from her and go to bed alone. Not without a night filled with dreams of his blond seductress who tasted as sweet as she smelled.

Before he could even draw his mouth away, however, to ask her if she wanted to make those dreams a reality, she jerked away. He saw her eyes widen and her mouth part in a half shriek just before something crashed into the back of his head with a painful thud.

Then everything went black.

5

"OH, MY GOD, Aunt Hildy, you knocked him out!"

Gwen crouched beside the secret agent sprawled on the faded linoleum floor of her kitchen. His eyes were closed, his lashes resting on his cheeks. As he'd fallen, he'd struck the table, tipping over his bottle, spilling water everywhere. So now he was both unconscious *and* lying in a sizable puddle.

Through his parted lips, he drew in a ragged breath. He was alive, at least. But his body remained limp. She shivered, both from concern, and because the room had suddenly become terribly chilly. Looking at Hildy, she asked, "What were you *thinking?*"

"I was saving you, dear. I got that bad man with this."

Gwen gaped as Hildy held up one leg from a pair of thick, old-lady support hose. The triple-strength nylon was bulging and misshapen, obviously filled with something heavy. Though her aunt held it high in her hand, the toe nearly touched the floor. "Rolled pennies. I keep this sucker in my bedside table. Learned that trick years ago. You'll never guess who taught me."

No, and she wasn't going to try. Especially not now, when there was an unconscious federal agent on her kitchen floor, and possibly an international arms dealer sleeping two floors above.

"Didn't have time to dig in my hope chest for my bean shooter," the woman continued. "But this did all right."

Bean shooter. Gwen groaned, knowing enough of Hildy's slang to know she was referring to her antique gun. Gwen had hoped she'd lost the thing. "Why would you do such a thing?"

"Moe told me there was a bad man here in the kitchen."

Moe. Six Fingers Moe. One of the ghosts her aunt considered her best friends, living or dead. Good lord. "Aunt Hildy..."

Suddenly, her aunt cocked a head sideways and frowned ferociously. "I do *not* need a hearing aid!"

"What?"

"Moe says I need a hearing aid, and now he's laughing."

Laughing ghosts. Unconscious spies. A crazy Halloween night at a haunted inn. Her life had turned into a bad B-movie.

Gwen closed her eyes, willing herself to open them and see only the ceiling of her room. This wasn't real. She had to have fallen asleep and was now in the middle of an incredibly intense dream. But when she opened her eyes she recognized the kitchen.

Aunt Hildy was shaking a bony fist in the air and glaring at the air above her head. "It's not funny. This is your fault."

On the floor, Miles Stone continued to lie in silence. Gorgeous, mysterious, dark and handsome. As still as a rock. And armed. And likely to be very ticked off when he woke up.

No, not a dream. This was a pure, undiluted nightmare. Not quite Freddy Krueger level, but pretty darn close.

Thinking back to the CPR classes she'd taken during her Girl Scout days, she scrambled to remember what one did to help an unconscious person. She touched Miles's neck, feeling a strong, steady pulse. Breathing a sigh of relief, she gently tilted his head. She bit her lip when her fingers brushed against a sizable lump on the back of his skull. "You could have killed him."

"Oh, my goodness," Hildy said, drawing her shaking hand up to her lips. "Moe swears he didn't say *bad* man. He said *G-man*. He woke me up to tell me there was a *G-man* in the kitchen."

Gwen carefully placed the man's head back on the floor then hurried to the refrigerator, still shivering in the chilly air of the kitchen. She grabbed a handful of ice, wrapped it in a towel and returned to Miles's side.

"That's why Moe's laughing. I pasted a G-man. Haven't done that since I was a girl." Hildy didn't sound too dismayed. In fact, an amused grin played about her lips.

"I should call for help." Gwen held the ice against the lump, thinking how fortunate it was that Miles had such thick brown hair. Perhaps it was sufficient cushion to prevent serious injury when struck by little old ladies armed with pennies.

Then again, her great-aunt was pretty strong. She'd once escaped a Chicago cop with a sharp elbow to the throat.

Hildy walked over and looked down at Miles, squinting to make out his features since she wasn't wearing her glasses. She hunkered down beside him, taking stock of his dark clothes, his long, lean body. "Nice." She looked up and obviously noticed Gwen's disapproval. "Come on, admit it. You think he's a hottie, too. Otherwise you wouldn't have been kissing him."

Gwen had hoped Aunt Hildy hadn't noticed that part, since she'd approached Miles from behind. She should have known better. Hildy was like a bloodhound when it came to sniffing out anything that hinted at romance. Particularly where Gwen was concerned. Hildy's skills apparently hadn't grown rusty with disuse. "Well, maybe so, but it's not nice to ogle an unconscious, helpless man."

"That's the best way to ogle them," Hildy replied with an unrepentant shrug. "'Specially when they're naked." She reached for Miles's sleeve.

"You're not taking his clothes off!"

"Of course I'm not. Though he is getting wet." She pointed to the puddle and gave Gwen a hopeful glance.

"No."

Hildy shrugged. "Never mind. I only wanted to check out this scar." She peered at Miles's hand, raising it toward the light so Gwen could also look at the curved, puckered flesh. "Bet he got shot. Or maybe he was in a knife fight. Or maybe he was tortured. Burned with cigarettes while tied down and forced to listen to William Shatner singing 'Mr. Tambourine Man.'"

Before Gwen could reply, or so much as chuckle at her aunt's typical twisting train of thought, Hildy continued. "Hmm...not bad." She lowered his hand and took a closer look at his face. "He is good-looking for a G-man. Big. Looks more like a bruno."

"His name is Miles. Miles Stone." Gwen said.

"I didn't mean Bruno was his *name.* I meant he looks more like an enforcer than a copper."

"A copper?"

"Yeah. Moe says he's not completely sure this guy is a G-man...you know, an FBI agent. But he's got something to do with the law. He could be a bull, a john, a private dick." When Gwen just stared at the old woman, Hildy put a hand on her hip, a picture of impatience. "Hammer and saw? A peeper?"

Speaking slowly, to cut through her great-aunt's obvious delight in whipping out the vocabulary of her youth, Gwen explained, "Aunt Hildy, this man is a federal agent. He's pursuing a very dangerous suspect. And you've just knocked him unconscious with a stocking full of pennies."

Her aunt pursed her lower lip and scrunched her nose. "Guess this isn't going to be good for business, huh?"

"It's not exactly legal, either." Not that being on the wrong side of the law had stopped Aunt Hildy in her younger days.

Hildy shrugged and rose to her feet, rubbing her back. "Not Moe's fault he didn't know what to call the guy. He don't know about the CIA cause he was dead before they got started up."

"He knows about Madonna," Gwen couldn't help muttering as she gently tapped on Miles's cheek to try to get him to wake up.

Either Hildy didn't hear her or she chose to ignore the comment. "If Moe had known about the CIA, he would have said there was a spook in here, and I wouldn't have worried. Spook doesn't sound anything like bad man."

No, but it does sound like kook. She instantly regretted the unkind thought. Her Aunt Hildy was *not* a kook. She was a darling, loveable, eccentric, funny old former gangster's moll who liked to talk to ghosts.

"G doesn't sound like bad, either," she replied. "Moe was right, you *do* need a hearing aid." When she heard the words come out of her own mouth, she couldn't believe she'd said them. She was agreeing with a ghost. Gwen Compton had officially lost it.

She returned her attention to their unconscious guest. "He's not coming to. We should call 9-1-1."

"Are you sure he's who he says he is?"

"I saw his ID. And he has a picture of the suspect." Gwen cast a glance toward the unconscious man's briefcase.

Hildy reacted with typical curiosity, grabbing the case and tugging it closer. "Let's make sure."

"Aunt Hildy, you leave that alone."

"No harm checking."

"*No.* No checking. We can't get involved with this. We just need to get him some medical attention." Quickly running over several options, she ruled out the most obvious one. There was too much at stake to pick up the phone and dial 9-1-1. An arriving ambulance, with sirens and lights, would wake up the house. Including the potentially dangerous man sleeping upstairs.

She couldn't risk it. Not while Miles was unconscious, unable to defend himself. Then she remembered...one of their guests was a doctor. But, for all she knew, the woman could very well be the mysterious Miss Jones that Miles had been talking about. She might be every bit as dangerous to Miles as the arms dealer.

Gwen closed her eyes, trying to remember every detail about the doctor. Thankfully, she immediately recalled how much she'd admired the lady's emerald necklace during the cocktail party. The dark-haired woman had been wearing it with a low-cut, square-necked dress. And most important...she'd seen no star-shaped birthmark.

"Aunt Hildy, can you please go up to the Lady in Red room and ask Dr. Wilson if she'll come down and help?"

"Lady in Red room," Hildy muttered, sounding almost as disgruntled as she did whenever her heel spurs started bothering her. "I hate that name. She was a stoolie."

"You're the one who *insisted* on the gangster theme."

Aunt Hildy didn't argue the point. They'd been over it too many times. Gwen had tried to talk her out of this gangster bed-and-breakfast idea, knowing how much the old woman's former associations had affected her life. Gwen had spent a lot of time trying to protect her only living relative from her scandalous past. But Hildy had been adamant, and she'd gotten her way. After all, though the money to improve it had been Gwen's, the house belonged to Aunt Hildy. She'd inherited it from Fat Lip Nathan, who had to have led a pretty lonely life if he'd willed his house to a woman he hadn't seen in over sixty years.

"All right, I'll go get the doctor," Hildy said, padding toward the door in her slippered feet, her long cotton nightgown swirling around her thin legs.

"And please, be careful. Don't wake up anyone else."

"I won't." Hildy smiled, as if she enjoyed the idea of being clandestine. "The only room on that side of the hall is Dillinger's Den. Is anybody in there?"

Gwen checked Miles's breathing again and gave a distracted nod. "Yes, so do be quiet. That Realtor is staying in there."

"Realtor?"

"The one who had this house listed for sale before the lawyer realized there was a living heir and tracked you down."

Miles stirred slightly, and she smoothed his hair off his brow in a comforting gesture. Then she glanced up at Aunt Hildy, who waited for clarification. "Remember? You know who I mean, your boyfriend Samuel's grandson. Mick Winchester."

AS HE SLOWLY regained consciousness, he became aware of an incredible softness against his cheek. And the smell of apples. Sweet, cinnamon apples. He tried to open his eyes, wanting to know the source of the delicious aroma, but even that tiny movement sent a shard of pain rushing through his skill.

"Are you awake?"

A soft voice. A husky voice. A feminine voice. A voice almost as intriguing as that smell. His mind crawled toward it, one mental step at a time, trying to climb out of the haze clouding his brain and making lead weights of his limbs.

"Ummm..." was the best he could do in response.

"Miles, I'm so sorry, I can't believe my aunt hit you."

The sweet-smelling woman's aunt had hit him? Didn't sound very dramatic, unless the aunt doubled as a heavyweight.

"She's old and protective. I don't imagine she realized a bag of pennies would be that heavy."

An *old lady* had caused this pain? With pennies? Not only sadly undramatic, it was beginning to sound downright pathetic.

"She thought you were someone else. And I can't imagine what she must have thought, walking in here and seeing us...kissing."

This time, his eyes flew open in spite of the pain. *Kissing?* He'd been kissing this delightful-sounding, delicious-smelling person? That was the type of thing he ought to know, right?

Unfortunately, he couldn't grab hold of a single thought, couldn't remember a damn thing because of the jackhammer pounding in his head. Something he regretted when his eyes cleared enough to let him take in the vision of a woman kneeling next to him.

Beautiful. Blond. Half-naked. With long, shining hair that lay tangled on his own chest because she was leaning over him. And perfect, magnificent breasts almost spilling out of a shimmery white gown, mere inches from his face.

He swallowed, hard, as all the blood not involved in making his temples pound descended due south. Funny how he could suddenly throb in two spots. His head. And his groin. Fortunately, she didn't appear to notice.

"Miles? Are you sure you're all right? I'm so sorry, I didn't see Aunt Hildy until it was too late." She glanced at her own fingers. "We were, uh, otherwise occupied."

Okay, what the hell had he forgotten? And, more important, how would she react if he leaned just a little bit closer and tasted that sweet, tempting curve? Because right now, all he could think about was sliding his tongue under the fabric, teasing that dark, puckered nipple with his lips and pulling one of her legs over his hips to straddle him.

If only he didn't feel as though someone had buried an ax behind his ears. "Where am I?" His tongue felt thick and heavy in his mouth, the headache increasing with each word he spoke.

"You're in the kitchen of the Little Bohemie Inn," the blond vision replied. "Don't you remember?"

"No."

She nibbled at her lip, reminding him of how much he liked kissing women with sultry, pouty bottom lips. At least, he thought he did. For some reason, he wasn't entirely sure. Not sure of anything, actually.

"You were unconscious for a few minutes. It's natural that you might be a little confused." She glanced around the room and lowered her voice. "Do you remember why you're here at the inn?"

He tried to shake his head, then thought better of it. "No, I don't. Christ, I don't remember much of anything."

A flash of disappointment tugged her brow down and he imagined how that must have sounded. If he'd been kissing her, he must *know* her. If not, they'd had a fast-moving acquaintance.

"You might need a minute or two for your head to clear."

He didn't know which of them she was trying to convince, but he appreciated the concern, again wondering how well he knew her. While her face sparked something deep inside his brain—something instinctive and elemental—he couldn't have spoken her name if someone put a gun to his head.

"Let me help you get that jacket off," she continued in that low, sultry whisper, as if afraid someone might overhear. "I'm nervous about you lying here with your gun underneath you."

Holy crap. A gun. He had a gun? Why would he have a gun?

"I'm armed?"

She nodded, nibbling her lip.

"You're sure?"

"Shh." She looked around again. "Keep your voice down. You're lying here, exposed and vulnerable."

Exposed? He shifted his eyes, checking everything out, making sure nothing was...er...left undone. Considering the world-class hard-on he'd been sporting since she'd leaned over him, he figured he'd have noticed if his pants weren't fastened. The room wasn't exactly warm, and he definitely wasn't feeling a draft. In fact, that particular area of his anatomy was getting damned hot.

"You showed it to me."

Showed *it?* His brow shot up. "I did?"

She nodded. "It wasn't very big."

Bullshit.

"Your gun, I mean," she clarified quickly, a faint blush the only indication that she'd correctly interpreted the half offended, half disbelieving expression on his face. "I was talking about the gun. You're lying on it. So you should probably take your jacket off."

"All right." Though the pain was beginning to recede until it resembled a butcher knife rather than a hatchet in his brain, he still cringed as he lifted his shoulders to remove the jacket.

Her comments about being "exposed" and "showing it" might have been made in perfect innocence. But he couldn't help risking another quick lap check. All clear. Except for the continued discomfort of a pair of pants that, like the Grinch's heart, suddenly felt two sizes too small.

She helped him slip out of the jacket, her body coming incredibly close to brushing against his. All his senses perked right up, conscious of the brush of her hair against his face, the sweet scent of her skin, the husky rhythm of her heavily indrawn breaths.

An inch. One inch closer and she'd be almost lying across his lap while she pushed the jacket off one shoulder and reached around to tug it out from under him. One inch and all that would keep them apart would be her silky white gown, his own dark clothes, and a headache the size of Milwaukee.

She pulled away, as if feeling the same flash of heated awareness. Tossing his jacket onto a chair, she turned a deeper shade of pink as he watched her, still trying to figure out just what had happened. Where it had happened. Why it had happened. And when it could happen again.

Unfortunately, without the leather coat as a barrier, he quickly became aware of a cold, wet sensation spreading on his back. "Am I lying in something? I'm getting wet. You sure your aunt didn't bash me with a snow globe?"

"Sorry. You tipped over a bottle of water when you fell."

"Great," he said with a heavy sigh. "I'm soaked." Not giving it another thought, he carefully sat up and reached for the waistband of his black jeans. He tugged the bottom of his lightweight black sweater out and began pulling it up.

"What are you doing?"

Given the note of near panic in her voice as she watched him undress, he had the feeling he and the blond one hadn't been about to progress from kissing to removing clothing. Too bad. He'd half hoped they'd been heading toward having wild sex on the kitchen table. That might have made up for him getting knocked out by a penny-armed granny. It also might have given him something to look forward to when his brain stopped throbbing and started working again.

"I'm soaked." His tone told her he was in no mood to argue over her delicate sensibilities. She watched, lips parted as she drew in deep breaths. She was all pink and flushed. So damned wide-eyed and innocent, her pulse beating wildly in her neck.

He suddenly had an almost uncontrollable impulse to growl, low in his throat, and gently nip at that neck. He wanted to taste her sweet skin, to feel her pulse beating against his tongue as he savored her.

Later. Definitely later.

She didn't help him tug the shirt off at first, maintaining a physical and mental distance. But when he tried to tug the sweater over his head, it scraped painfully against a boulder growing out of the back of his skull. He groaned.

"Let me help you," she insisted, sounding disgruntled.

She didn't act disgruntled, though. In fact, her hands almost lingered as she tugged the fabric free of his shoulders. He felt her fingers move lightly across his bare chest, and he shivered a bit in instinctive reaction. Then she slid her hands under the turtle neckline and eased it over his head.

"Better," he murmured.

"Better," she repeated, still kneeling close. So close he could see the flecks of gold in her beautiful amber irises, could see her gaze drop to his lips. To his shoulders. To his bare chest and stomach.

The throbbing in his groin became more urgent than the one in his head. Her stare held such heat. Such sensual *want*. Without thinking, he reached out and tangled his fingers in her hair, tugging her close. "I wanna kiss you."

"But your head..."

"It'll damn well be worth the pain."

She didn't pull away, silently inviting him to proceed. He did. He tugged her forward, tightening his fingers in her hair, curling them around her head and holding her close while he dragged her mouth to his. Her lips parted, and their tongues met in a lazy, gentle mating of two people in tune with each other, familiar with each other's tastes, likes and dislikes.

They'd done this before, but not enough. Not nearly enough.

It wasn't until she lifted her hands to tangle in his hair that he remembered the painful lump. Her fingers brushed against it and he gave a small jerk. Wincing, he watched her pull away.

"I'm so sorry! Are you all right?"

"Yeah. I'm fine. Just a killer headache."

At least, he thought he was fine. But there was more than a pounding in his head making him feel unsettled, uncomfortable. Like something was hovering right out of reach, but he didn't even know what it was he sought.

Then he realized something. Something that made him stop and think. Really think.

In those few moments of trying to figure out where he was, and wondering about the nature of his relationship with the luscious blonde in the white nightgown—who she was, how well they knew each other—he hadn't quite grasped the real problem. The main thing he'd forgotten. The question of the hour.

Who the hell was *he?*

6

MICK WINCHESTER was a light sleeper. Particularly when he was sleeping alone, in a great big bed, and there was an irresistible redhead occupying the next room. The lady doctor from out of town had been cool during cocktails...but that's just because she hadn't gotten to know him yet.

Since he'd gone to bed thinking about her, sleep proved elusive. So he was awake to hear a soft knock on the door to the next room. He grabbed a pair of jeans and tugged them up over his hips. Not bothering to fasten them all the way, he padded over to look out into the hall. "Everything all right?"

He spied the elderly owner of the inn talking with the doctor. The doctor who was scantily clad in a red silk teddy. He grinned as she stepped behind the door frame, discreetly removing herself from his view. "Let me dress and I'll come down," she whispered.

"What's wrong?" he asked after the other door clicked shut.

Hildy Compton might be pushing ninety, but she was a wicked flirt. "Sleeping alone doesn't sit right with you, does it, Mr. Winchester?" She gave him a visual once-over that made him laugh instead of making him dive for his shirt. Hildy was harmless. So far, she hadn't pinched his butt or anything, though he didn't trust her enough to turn his back.

"Not really," he admitted.

"What happened to the little chickie you were supposed to bring with you this weekend?"

He didn't want to discuss the little chickie, a telephone solicitor he'd been dating for a few weeks. They'd planned to spend the weekend at the inn, since the first time they'd met had been here at his party *last* Halloween. Then, they'd both been with other people. Now, they were both single again. Mainly because she couldn't understand any word longer than two syllables. And because he always hung up on telephone solicitors.

"Mrs. Compton, is someone hurt?"

She nodded, then lowered her voice to whisper, "There's a secret agent man knocked out cold in the kitchen."

Of all things he expected to hear, this definitely wasn't on the top ten list. "An unconscious secret agent," he repeated, wondering if the old lady had gone off her meds. Or her rocker.

"Yep. It's very hush-hush. You can't tell the doctor who he is—she's a stranger. But I'll tell you because Gwen likes you. She'd have to, otherwise, I expect she'd have bloodied your nose for putting the moves on her one too many times."

Old news. Once she'd made it clear she wasn't interested, he and Gwen had developed a friendship. He liked her. She was hot, but even he recognized she wasn't his type. "Hildy, are you feeling all right? Maybe the doctor should check you out."

"No thanks," the old lady sniffed. "I'm of sound mind *and* body. Just ask your grandpa."

Mick scrunched his eyes shut at the quick mental image her words invoked. The old woman testing the springs in his eighty-seven-year-old grandfather's bed. Not someplace he wanted to go.

"I'm ready." The doctor returned, wearing a tight sweater and jeans that hugged some mouthwatering curves.

"Do you need help?"

She cast a quick, assessing glance over his naked chest and unfastened jeans. Though she went for cool dismissal, he couldn't miss the flush rising in her cheeks. "I can handle it. Mrs. Compton says she struck someone and he's unconscious."

The old lady had knocked out the secret agent? Uh-huh. "All the same, maybe I'll come, too. Do you know this person's name?"

The old lady scrunched her brow. "Can't recall. Gwen mentioned it." Then she snickered. "But I don't know how much the two of them could have talked with his lips stuck to hers."

Ahh...now this was getting interesting. He'd like to meet the man who could break through Gwen's cool, reserved facade. "I'll be down in a minute. Let me dress."

He turned to walk away, overhearing the last bit of Hildy's conversation with the doctor. "Handsome devil he is."

"Mr. Winchester?" the doctor asked, making Mick smile.

"Him, too. But I meant the stone-cold bit of goods in the kitchen. He's tall. With thick, dark hair. Good chin. Got a wicked, half-circle scar on his left hand, so he's the dangerous type, I think." Her voice suddenly grew louder, as if she wanted Mick to hear. "I just remembered his name. It's Miles Stone."

Stone. Miles Stone. The name seemed familiar, and not only because it was pretty awful. How much would a set of parents have to dislike their own offspring to saddle him with such a name?

Mick tugged a sweatshirt over his shoulders. Then he froze, a memory tickling in the back of his brain. Tall. Dark hair. A half-circle scar on his hand. And a name Mick had made up for his cousin to use at his party *last* Halloween. "No, it's impossible."

Or maybe it wasn't.

Not giving it another thought, he raced down the stairs toward the kitchen, arriving in time to hear Hildy exclaim, "You mean he's got amnesia? He doesn't know who the heck he is?"

From impossible to frigging surreal. Mick watched, his mouth agape, taking in the scene. His cousin Jared *was* the man sitting on the kitchen floor, looking up at the three women. Jared was bare-chested, wide-eyed and clutching his head. His expression vacillated between looking with visual hunger at the nightgown-clad Gwen Compton, and merely looking mad as hell. He was also demanding to know who and where he was.

Some instinct made Mick duck back out of the room. "This has gotta be a gag." Jared was playing a Halloween prank. He must have found out Mick was at the inn and set this up. He'd been threatening retaliation against Mick for ages, ever since the strippers-at-the-book-signing incident. It could even go back as far as their childhood years, to the time Mick had removed a ladder, leaving his cousin stranded on the roof for five hours.

Jared still blamed him for his problem with heights.

He chuckled. Damn, it was good to have the fun, joke-playing Jared back. The past few times he'd seen him, his cousin had been so bloody intense and brooding. It was about time he'd remembered he had a sense of humor. Judging by the way he'd been looking at Gwen, he'd rediscovered his libido, too.

Mick wondered how long Jared would carry on with the joke now that he'd been distracted by his sexy hostess. Speaking of which...he peeked around the doorjamb again. His cousin still stared intently at the blonde, ignoring the attractive doctor hovering over him. He had eyes for no one but Gwen, inhaling her with every glance, offering her that mysterious half smile that had been known to drive women crazy since he'd been a teenager.

Mick recognized that look: Jared when intrigued. It was good to see it. He hoped his real cousin was back for good and that the brooding introvert was long gone.

Chuckling softly, he decided to do some reconnaissance, starting by searching Jared's car. If this was a joke, he needed to prepare himself. And plan his revenge.

If it wasn't a joke, and his cousin really was hurt—well, judging by the way Jared was reacting to the innkeeper, Mick had the feeling he was in pretty capable hands.

Either way, it was shaping up to be a damned entertaining Halloween weekend.

GWEN WISHED the doctor, Anne Wilson, wasn't wearing a high-necked sweater—she'd like to get another look to make sure she saw no signs of a birthmark. Unfortunately, she had to rely on her memory from earlier in the evening.

She did like the efficient, concerned way Dr. Wilson examined their unexpected patient. She also liked that the attractive woman didn't openly drool over that patient's bare, muscle-rippled chest, or his strong, broad-as-a-board shoulders. Gwen found herself having to look away, wishing he'd put his wet shirt back on. Clothed, the man was striking, but at least manageable. Unclothed, he could rock the entire world. Or, at the very least, her little corner of it.

Dr. Wilson ran a series of quick tests, paying close attention to Miles's reflexive responses, his pupils and the injury on the back of his head. Though Gwen had offered to help him move into the parlor, for more light, they hadn't needed to. Somehow, the overhead kitchen fixture had started working again once Hildy had fiddled with the switch.

Gwen still wasn't convinced this was all real, and that she wasn't asleep in her bed, having dreamed the whole situation. Hearing him admit he didn't know who he was had been as shocking and dramatic as the kiss they'd shared minutes before. She was still stunned—from the kiss, and from his apparent amnesia. Not to mention the whole secret agent thing.

She'd read about amnesia, seen it in the movies, but had never witnessed it firsthand. There was no denying, however, that Miles had no clue who or where he was. He'd said as much, the minute their last kiss had ended. She'd had time to tell him only her name—and his—before Hildy had returned with the doctor.

"You're sure you don't want to go to the hospital?" the doctor asked as she finished her examination. "You probably have a slight concussion."

"But he doesn't need stitches." Hildy sounded defensive, probably feeling guilty about her assault. "You said my pennies didn't break the skin."

The doctor looked amused. Miles...less so.

"I don't want to go to a hospital," he stated. "I just need aspirin for the pain. Oh, yes, and a pill to pop my memories back into my head would be nice."

The doctor chuckled. "No magic pill. Sorry. But don't worry, this type of thing is not that unusual. A brief period of memory loss isn't uncommon after a head injury involving a bout of unconsciousness. I'll lay money that tomorrow morning everything will fall back into place." Then she crossed her arms. "But I was serious about the concussion. Someone needs to watch you for a while. A hospital would be the best solution."

"Gwen will watch him," Hildy piped in.

"Of course we will," Gwen added. She and her aunt were responsible for this mess. Until he remembered why he was here, she wasn't leaving Agent Stone alone in this house. Even if he'd been b.s.'ing her about who he was and why he was here, he'd still been injured in *her* kitchen, by *her* relative. She owed him something.

If he was telling the truth, he could be in danger, at the mercy of someone. A Russian terrorist. *Or a wicked innkeeper.*

He studied her with those dark, knowing eyes, and she wondered just what she'd let herself in for. His voice silky and loaded with meaning, he asked, "You'll stay with me all night?"

Gwen gulped, wondering how her aunt or the doctor could miss his implication. "Absolutely." She cleared her throat, wondering who that weak-sounding stranger who'd answered had been. Squaring her shoulders, she clarified, "My aunt and I will take shifts."

"Well, normally I wouldn't mind," Hildy said. Then, she smiled like a Cheshire cat, her sharp eyes not missing a thing in spite of her advanced age. She'd undoubtedly noticed the heat between Gwen and the handsome stranger. "But tonight I am so tired." She rubbed her hip, trying to look pitiful, but an excited glimmer in her eyes gave her away. "My niece looks wide-awake, though. She'll take good care of you, won't you, Gwen?" When Gwen frowned, Hildy stepped closer. "After all, remember the old poem? You have Miles to *do* before you sleep?"

Gwen groaned. "It's *go,* Hildy," she muttered between clenched teeth. But it didn't matter. Even the doctor, a stranger, couldn't miss that blatant a suggestion. The woman's shoulders shook as she laughed.

Miles wasn't laughing. He was, however, smiling. Smiling like a man who had a long night of pleasure to look forward to, rather than a long night of pain and card games, which was what Gwen had envisioned. Had *forced* herself to envision.

"So, I take it you and I know each other rather well, Miss Compton?" he asked, his tone silky.

Aunt Hildy answered. "Nope. You're complete strangers. That's what makes it so funny."

Gwen willed a zipper to miraculously appear over her querulous old relative's mouth, but her luck wasn't that good.

"Funny, why?" Miles asked.

"Well, funny that you two were lip-locked before I brained you. Gwen here hasn't been that close to a man in more'n a year. Way too long for a woman with strong...needs."

Oh, God, this had to be a nightmare. *Please don't let my eighty-five-year-old great-aunt be discussing my sexual needs with a complete stranger.*

This time, Miles did laugh. "I think I'm lucky I just got bashed with a bag of pennies, Ms. Compton," he told Hildy with a rueful shake of his head. "I suspect you have a lot more dangerous tricks up your sleeve."

Hildy preened. "I've got a story or two."

That did it. "No," Gwen said, stepping close to gently take Hildy's arm. "No stories tonight, love."

Hildy loved to chat. Gwen used to love to listen, would get caught up in the drama, the danger, the thrill, even the gruesome details of Hildy's criminal associates. But Hildy didn't realize that not everyone found her past as amusing as she did. One day, Gwen feared, someone would use it against her. To expose her, hurt her, upset the peaceful life they'd created here. Upset the delicate mental state Hildy had worked so hard to achieve and Gwen tried so hard to protect. "Aunt Hildy, I really think you should go to bed now."

"All right. And I think *you* should go to bed, too," the old woman replied with a wink at the injured man. "She can make sure you're not loopy in the head from concussion." She leaned close and whispered in a voice loud enough to wake the ghosts in the basement. "And once you're sure you're okay, you make sure to thank her properly for her help."

This time, Dr. Wilson snorted, not even attempting to hide her amusement. "All right then, I'll see you tomorrow," she said. "Miss Compton, do you have some acetaminophen you can give him?"

Gwen had already retrieved it. Miles took the bottle from her hand, his fingers lingering against hers one second longer than necessary. He dumped a few tablets into his palm and accepted a glass of water, which Hildy had filled for him.

"Fine. But no more than that," the doctor cautioned. Then she turned and walked toward the doorway.

Gwen followed her into the hall, leaving Hildy to say good-night to Miles. She wanted to talk to the doctor, but she also wanted to escape Miles's amused—but deeply knowing—stare.

Surprisingly, Mick Winchester stood right outside the door. She hadn't realized he'd come downstairs. Dr. Wilson obviously hadn't, either. A faint flush crawled up the woman's pretty face, pinkening her pale cheeks.

Ahh...another hapless female fell victim to Mick's boyish charm and smart-ass grin. She almost chuckled, liking that the shoe was suddenly on the other foot. For a confirmed bachelor and self-confessed ladies' man, Mick was a likable guy, even if he was too flirtatious for her taste. The lady doctor could do worse if she was looking for a playmate during her holiday weekend.

"Well?" Mick asked.

Dr. Wilson quickly explained her diagnosis.

Mick's eyes widened and he shook his head in disbelief. "You're saying Hildy knocked out a grown man with a bunch of pennies? God, this is too bizarre to be anything but a joke. He's faking the amnesia, right?"

The doctor shook her head. "I don't think so. It's not unusual for there to be some mental confusion when someone's knocked out cold with a blow to the head. I'm sure he'll remember and will laugh over this in the morning. These cases aren't as dramatic as in the movies. They're generally short-lived...hours, at most. I feel sure he'll be fine soon."

Mick didn't look convinced. He glanced at his hand, in which he held a wallet—probably his own—and a wrinkled, water-stained manila envelope. Gwen couldn't make out any writing on the envelope, just a jack-o'-lantern sticker. The wallet was easier to understand. He'd probably grabbed it in case he'd had to make an emergency trip to the hospital. That didn't surprise her. For a shameless ladies' man, Mick was a pretty nice guy.

"You're *sure* he's not faking?" he asked Dr. Wilson.

"I'm sure about the injury to his head. And the bruise on his shoulder from where he struck a chair while falling."

The pretty doctor lifted a hand to scrape a long strand of hair away from her face. Mick's concern for the man in the kitchen seemed to be momentarily tempered by his fascination with the way the woman's shirt pulled tighter against her body as she moved. He watched her with palpable interest.

Gwen almost laughed again. *The randy flirt.* She didn't know whether to be amused or relieved that he hadn't commented on her own skimpy nightie. Though, of course, he had noticed it. She'd seen him give her a thorough once-over when she'd exited the kitchen.

"So, you had a chance to talk with this man before he was injured?" he asked her once he'd finally stopped watching Dr. Wilson with frank appreciation in his eyes.

Talk? Oh, yeah, they'd talked. Her pulse quickened as she remembered the conversation she'd shared with Miles. How she could have been so totally lost to time and place, to propriety and her own self-preservation, she didn't know. All she knew was that if her Aunt Hildy hadn't knocked the man out, she might not have left the kitchen after he'd kissed her good-night.

At least, she might not have left alone. Because in his arms, for those last few seconds before he'd crumpled to the floor, she'd contemplated inviting him to come upstairs with her. If not for Hildy, they might right now be involved in the kind of erotic bedroom activities she'd only ever fantasized about. In spite of having been with a few other men in her life, she'd sensed from the first that the intense, dark, handsome secret agent could make her feel things she'd never felt, try things she'd never tried.

How bizarre for a woman who'd grown so accustomed to playing it safe. How strange that she'd never doubted, not for one moment, how much he'd wanted her, in spite of the serious blow her self-confidence had taken during her last relationship.

How naughty that the very good-girl innkeeper, for one night had wanted to be very, *very* bad.

Too late now.

Then she thought of the hours stretching before them. She just as quickly forced that flash of speculation out of her mind. She'd be sitting up with him tonight as a babysitter. Nothing else. The man probably had a concussion, for God's sake. He couldn't remember his own name, much less hers! And he certainly wouldn't be up to fulfilling the erotic fantasies of a lonely woman while sporting a colossal headache.

Pity.

Mick seemed to notice the way she'd gotten lost in her own thoughts. A slight smile curved his lips, as if he knew what she was thinking. She cleared her throat, finally remembering his question. "We spoke briefly."

"Uh-huh." Then he crossed his arms and leaned on the banister. "And he told you his name?"

She nodded.

"Did he say anything else?"

The doctor still stood there, listening to their conversation, but Gwen wasn't sure she was doing it out of concern for her patient. No, Dr. Wilson had been surreptitiously doing some looking of her own in the past few moments. At Mick.

"Not really." Then she frowned, remembering something. "It's strange, Aunt Hildy says she didn't check him in, but I can't ask him about it. Thankfully we do have a vacant room."

"Well, I think I'll go back upstairs," the doctor said. Then she looked at Mick. "Funny, I'm not as tired as I was when

I went to bed a couple of hours ago. Must be all the excitement. I might have to finish that brandy I took up with me after the cocktail hour, Miss Compton." But she never took her eyes off Mick. And Gwen saw a flash of something in her eyes. Interest? Maybe. Heat? Definitely. Perhaps even acceptance, though, as far as she could figure, no question had yet been asked.

Shockingly, Mick didn't offer to escort her to her room.

"Good night, Doctor," he murmured, looking regretful. "Gwen, can we talk for a minute?"

The doctor stiffened, probably as surprised as Gwen was. Mick let out an audible sigh as she walked away. He obviously realized he'd lost out on something.

"You must *really* want to talk," Gwen said. "You just gave up about as close to a sure thing as I've seen in a long time."

Mick gave her a cheeky wink. "The night's young. And I'm good at apologizing." Then he got serious. "I have something to tell you. Something about that stranger in the kitchen."

Her breath immediately caught. "What about him?"

"I know who he is."

Oh, lord. Aunt Hildy had said something. "Listen, Mick..."

"And I know why he didn't check in. He wouldn't, not right away, until he made sure it was safe. But I know why he's here, because he came to meet *me*."

This time, confusion made her tilt her head. "You?"

Lowering his voice, Mick leaned close.

"Yes. I'm his contact here in Derryville, Gwen. Agent Stone and I are working together."

7

OKAY, SO HIS NAME was Miles Stone, and for some reason he'd been in the kitchen of a bed-and-breakfast, making out with a gorgeous blonde in a negligee, when her old lady aunt had nailed him with a bag of pennies. He'd gone down for the count. And he'd come to with an empty memory bank and an ostrich egg-size lump on his skull, as well as the biggest bitch of a headache he'd ever experienced.

Or, so he thought, since he couldn't remember any previous headaches. Nor could he remember anything else. But at least the headache had faded in the hour since he'd taken the medicine and come upstairs to one of the bedrooms in this B & B.

He'd been dressed all in black. The beautiful innkeeper and her dotty aunt seemed nervous for some reason. And he'd supposedly been carrying a gun. So...he had a lot of questions.

Why did his own name, Miles Stone, ring no bells in his mind? What was he doing at a bed-and-breakfast with no luggage—as he'd discovered when he'd been escorted to this empty room. Why would he have a gun? Why wasn't he carrying a wallet in his back pocket? Why would Gwen Compton be so cautious, listening for every creak, peering around corners as she led him upstairs?

Why had they been making out in the kitchen when, by God, every molecule in his body screamed that he should have had her in a bed? Naked. Panting.

Maybe most important, who was she to him and how would she react if he picked up where they'd left off before the aunt had interfered?

Unfortunately, his companion didn't appear inclined to answer a damn thing. "You're sure you don't want me to try to find you something else to sleep in?" Gwen asked, her eyes shifting to stare everywhere in the room but at him, sitting in the bed with a sheet draped loosely over his legs and hips.

She'd scrounged up a robe somewhere and had covered up that skimpy white nightgown of hers. Too bad.

"I'm fine. And decent," he replied carelessly.

True. She couldn't see anything through the dark green sheet. Even if she could, he wasn't naked. He was apparently a boxer-briefs kinda guy. Thank goodness. He'd have hated to strip out of his black jeans and see tighty whities, or, God forbid, something hideous like a leopard-print thong. At least, whoever he was, he didn't dress like a loser.

But she'd stepped out of the room to let him undress, so she didn't know what his underwear of choice was. *Yet.* Since she'd returned, her cute little rear had been perched at the edge of a chair, as if she intended to flee if he moved off the bed.

"I'm fine, Miss Compton. Now, how about you and I stop staring at each other and get down to business?"

"I don't know what you mean."

He raised a disbelieving brow. Sure she didn't. There'd definitely been some mutual staring during their small talk about the weather, the inn and the merits of acetaminophen over aspirin when it came to concussions and penny-induced headaches. But every time he tried to make the conversation more informative, or more personal, she looked away and clammed up.

"I mean, let's cut to the chase," he said. "You're not telling me something. I want to know what it is."

She shook her head. "That's not a good idea. We just have to get you through the night. You should be able to sleep soon, it's been almost two hours since the, uh...unfortunate incident."

That was one way to put it.

"Your speech isn't slurred. Your eyes look normal. You seem well enough to go to sleep in another hour or so."

Leaving him wondering how they might fill that hour.

"And tomorrow you should wake up and remember everything."

He wasn't sure he liked the way she said *everything*. "What if I don't? Remember by tomorrow, I mean."

He regretted the question when he saw her stricken look.

"You have to remember. It's dangerous..."

"Dangerous?" He sat up straighter.

"I didn't mean to say that."

"You said it. Look, I've had enough of this. I might have a lump on my head and a lack of personal data at my disposal, but I'm not on my deathbed." Throwing the sheet back, he stepped out of the bed, not caring that she gasped at the sight of his body, clad only in his gray boxer-briefs.

Not giving her a chance to get up and leave, he walked around her and planted himself in front of the door. Crossing his arms in front of his chest, he merely looked at her. If she wanted out, she was gonna have to go through him. "Just because my memory's gone, doesn't mean I'm stupid. I know there's something more than meets the eye going on here. Start talking."

She stared up, not rising from her chair, as if her legs had suddenly turned to mush and she didn't trust herself to stand. She didn't touch him...not with her hands. But right now, standing with his waist at about the level of her head, he knew what was meeting *her* eye. She continued to look, with eyes full of hunger and heat, making no effort to disguise the way her lips parted and her breaths grew ragged.

The already palpable awareness between them skyrocketed.

Damn. Getting out of the bed had been a big tactical error. No way he could focus on getting answers, not when he couldn't even hide his reaction to her blatant interest.

She noticed that reaction. Considering the size of his hard-on, a person standing a block away could notice it.

Her body shook, her nipples puckering to twin peaks below her gown. His mouth went dry with want. Had he tasted that sweet spot? Had he sucked her nipples, rolled them on his tongue? Had he cupped her, licked her, sampled every inch of her?

Not knowing if it had happened was hell. Not knowing if it would happen *again* was worse.

A flush washed over her. She didn't appear to notice that one sleeve of her silky robe had slid down, baring her shoulder, the curve of her neck, and the low-cut neckline of her gown. Standing above her, he was unable to look away, imagining her touching him with her hands, her mouth, as well as with her hungry eyes.

In her lap, her fingers clenched together, inching higher, almost of their own will, toward the apex of her thighs. As if she had a need to fulfill. Even if she had to do it herself.

The thought sent even more blood rushing to his groin. And he gleaned one more fact about himself. He had a big...

"Don't you think you should get back into bed?" she asked, her final word almost a squeak.

Bed. Yeah. That'd work. If only it weren't abso-friggin'-lutely impossible. "You're killing me," he growled.

His world-class hard-on wasn't going away until he did something about it. Or until *she* did. Which couldn't happen. Until he knew who he was—if he was married, an escaped convict or a sex fiend—he could not touch her.

One thing was for sure. He was definitely straight. Because he could picture making love to this woman in more positions than you could find in the *Kama Sutra* and still not get enough of her.

The thought made him even harder. So hard, he nearly erupted out of his low-riding briefs.

"Oh, my God," she whispered, her jaw wide open. She stared at his crotch like he was some kind of dancer at a strip club.

Hell, maybe he *was*.

"I think you'd better get out of here," he said, his voice thick and hoarse, the words so painful he nearly had to rip them from his throat. He stepped away from the door, willing her to leave. When what he really wanted to do was to pull her close. Very close. To bury himself inside her and let all the confusion be washed away by raw, physical intimacy. "Go *now*."

Shaking her head, she stood to face him and sucked in a few deep, ragged breaths. "I can't leave you alone."

"I'm fine," he bit out between clenched teeth.

She squared her shoulders. "I'm not going anywhere. You can get back under the covers, and we can..."

Have wild, horny, sweaty, kinky sex.

"Talk. Or play cards. You just go back over there to your side of the room. Everything will be fine." He didn't know who she was trying to convince more with that weak, breathy voice...him or herself.

He'd tried to play the gentleman, tried to send her on her way untouched, safe and sound. She hadn't taken him up on his offer. So now all bets were off. "Okay. Suit yourself." Stepping closer until their bodies almost touched, he pressed each of his hands on the wall behind her head, effectively trapping her.

"But if you stay, we're going to pick up wherever we left off downstairs in the kitchen."

GWEN KNEW he was trying to intimidate her into leaving, for her own good. If he knew the truth—that his implied threat excited her more than it frightened her—he'd be the one in retreat. Because he didn't *mean* it. He wanted answers, not sex.

Well, okay, he probably wanted both. Correction, judging by the erection straining against his underwear, and, *oh, God,* nearly erupting from the top of them, he *definitely* wanted sex. But she'd lay money he wanted answers more. She certainly would, if the situation were reversed. She'd want to know who she was before she could even think about having hot, erotic sex with a stranger.

Then again, she wasn't a guy.

"You want to bring me up to speed on how far we'd progressed before we were so painfully interrupted?" His voice had returned to that sultry purr she remembered from earlier that night. His tone was sensuous and hypnotic. His stare equally so.

"W-we were saying goodnight."

He stepped closer, until his bare legs brushed against hers and one of his feet was between her own. "Sure we were."

She flattened herself as far as she could against the wall, fisting her hands to avoid throwing her arms around the poor man's neck and begging him to take her. Now. Hard. Right where they stood. Or on the bed. Or in the bathtub. Or all of the above.

Not the kind of thing one should do to a secret agent with a concussion and amnesia. Not when the bad guy could be pounding down the door any minute, catching them unprepared. Distracted. In the throws of ultimate physical pleasure. Damn, it almost seemed worth the risk when she thought of it in those terms.

"So, I'm to believe we were going to bed...separately?"

"We were," she said. "We just met tonight."

He thought about it. "Okay, I guess I can buy that. I can't imagine even a blow to the head could make me forget you if we knew each other more...intimately." He looked down, his gaze resting on the gaping vee of her robe, where the glittery, beaded bodice of her nightgown was exposed. "We obviously hit it off."

She nodded. "Yes, we did." Clearing her throat she said, "But that doesn't matter now. We have to make sure you're okay tonight and everything will be fine tomorrow. You'll get your memory back. You'll do what you came here to do. Then you'll go." *Taking the arms dealer sleeping upstairs with you.*

And maybe coming back for a visit in the future, when this was all over. God, she'd give a year off her life if he'd come back so they could finish what they'd started. Particularly now, when she'd seen the physical evidence of what he had to offer.

A lot.

His eyes narrowed. "What I came here to do. You mean, beyond this?" He pressed against her suggestively. His tight boxers and her nightwear were the only things separating the hungriest parts of them both. "*Is* there anything beyond this?"

No. She didn't think there was. Hadn't thought so ever since she'd seen him get out of that bed, her body instantly responding. Without a touch, merely at the sight of him, she'd gotten so aroused she'd barely trusted herself to stand up.

He moved again, brushing his hips against hers in an agonizing sexual tease, coaxing a hopeless whimper from her mouth. How could he know her so well when he didn't know her at all? Was she so easy to read, so pathetic a female that he had been able to tell just by looking at her how much she wanted him? Had wanted him since she first set eyes on him?

"We can't." That sounded about as strong-willed as a teenager who'd already climbed into the back of a car with her boyfriend. *We can't. We mustn't. We shouldn't. Take me, baby!*

He ignored her, moving his hands lower on the wall until his forearms touched her shoulders and his fingers teased a few long strands of her hair. She sighed. Obviously hearing the sound, he lowered his mouth to her throat, tasting her skin, breathing deeply as if he couldn't get enough of her scent.

Her brain screamed *danger*. Her body said *to hell with it*.

"So," he continued as he moved higher, sliding his tongue on her neck as if testing the fluttering of her pulse. "What am I doing here, Gwen?" Another nip. Another tiny flick of his tongue. Another question. "What haven't you told me?"

She couldn't think, could barely breathe, could hardly remember her own name at this point.

"Come on, angel. Let's just get it out in the open and

move on." He kissed higher, sucking her earlobe into his mouth and nibbling it so lightly she shivered with sensation.

"Tell me." He punctuated the command by lowering his hand to trail his fingers along the neckline of her gown, tracing a path on the sensitive skin above her breast. *"Tell me."*

Resistance was futile. Gwen caved in like a guilty suspect being interrogated by Sipowicz on *NYPD Blue.* Or like a counterspy being seduced into talking by James Bond. That was probably closer to the truth. Her words came out in a rush, on one long, exhaled breath. "You're a secret agent and you're chasing a Russian arms dealer and his buyer and you were supposed to meet your local contact tonight, but he knows you're hurt, so he's outside making sure the perimeter is secure. I'm to stay here with you to make sure you're all right and if you stop touching me, I think I'll die."

There. All said. And obviously shocking, because he stopped the sensual assault and merely looked at her with an open jaw and wide eyes. She waited, wondering if he'd remember, if hearing the truth would put his memories back where they belonged.

He finally shook his head and stepped back, swiping a hand through his hair as he absorbed her words. Then he tsked.

"That's the stupidest story I have ever heard."

AS IMPOSSIBLE as it seemed, Gwen's ridiculous explanation cut through the haze of lust in Miles's brain, reminding him of who and where he was. Well, at least *where* he was. The who remained up for debate. "That sounded like a bad movie script."

She shot him a look that held both irritation and a hint of

disappointment that he'd stepped away from her, breaking the sensual aura between them. Irritation apparently won out. With a firm set of her chin, she grabbed a briefcase and tossed it on to the bed. She didn't ask permission before opening it. Not that he'd have given it—he didn't recognize the damn briefcase and had no idea whether it was his or not.

"Well, then, why are you carrying these? Most average guys or traveling salesmen don't have dossiers on Russian killers, crime scene photos, aerial maps or encoded messages, do they?"

"I've fallen into a *Mission Impossible* movie," he muttered. Still, he couldn't resist stepping closer, watching as she pulled files, papers, reports and photos from the case. She tossed him a file and he caught it in midair.

"Read it."

"It's in another language," he said, still not willing to accept her story as truth.

"Humor me."

So he did. He opened the file and something in his brain sparked, told him he knew this, had seen it before. He began to read aloud from a Moscow police report, detailing a series of break-ins that had preceded a 1972 murder case.

She crossed her arms and raised a brow in triumph. "You read and speak Russian."

"So does Baryshnikov," he shot back. "That doesn't make him a secret agent any more than it makes me a ballet dancer."

God, at least he *hoped* not. No. No frigging way was he a ballet dancer. Just to be sure, he tried to conjure up some music in his mind. All he came back with was classic Stones, with some Metallica thrown in. Nothing remotely balletlike. Thank God.

He tossed the file back into the briefcase. "Where's this so-called local connection of mine?"

"He's outside, but we spoke while you were in the kitchen." She nibbled her lip. "I'll admit, I was skeptical of you and your story. But I've known Mick since I moved here and he confirmed your identity. He's a real estate agent."

He snorted with laughter. "Oh, yeah, there's a great backup. What's he gonna do, help the killer get low-rate financing for his next missile? Refer him to Illinois Van Lines to transport his cache of weapons?"

"Ha ha."

"I think I heard about a counterespionage school for Realtors in California. Handgun training and no closing costs."

"I liked you better when you were threatening to kill me," she muttered, obviously not enjoying his amusement.

He paused. "I threatened to kill you? What'd you do?"

Raising a brow, as if daring him to laugh again, she replied, "I kissed you."

He immediately lowered his voice, picturing the moment, picturing her in his arms, their bodies entwined, his fingers tangling in her hair and her hands on his hips. "Did I like it?"

She pursed her lips and purred, "You loved it."

He swallowed hard. Yeah. Of course he would have loved it. "So, do you usually kiss the men who threaten to kill you?"

"I knew you were kidding. Besides, it made sense at the time," she answered with a shrug.

"Maybe having a realtor be my backup made sense to me at some point, too," he conceded.

"Mick's got a family history going back a hundred years around here. He knows everyone and everyone knows him. Who better to provide information on this town to the feds?" Not giving him another chance to shoot down her theory, she grabbed two more items from the briefcase and held them up. An identification card with a photo, plus a badge. "And there are these."

The badge was a tougher stumbling block than the language thing. Plus, that *was* his picture on an ID card—though he looked younger in it. "What's the Shop?" he asked.

"You tell me."

He didn't speak, trying hard to focus his thoughts, grab pieces of truth out of his uncooperative mind. And there, deep in his lost memory, he did find reference to a top-secret government agency called the Shop. He didn't know why he had the knowledge, but there was no doubt he did.

Probably the most damning thing of all, though, was that something about Gwen's story had begun to ring true. The police files and badge had felt familiar in his hands. He had the feeling a gun would, too.

And what reason would there be for him to carry around those documents—coroner's reports and photos of crime scenes that should have induced shock, but brought out an almost analytical curiosity instead? He again glanced at the items in the briefcase with an almost surreal sense of déjà vu, knowing he'd seen them before. That he'd put them there. That he'd pored over them. That if he sat down and wrote something, the handwriting would match the notations made in red on the folders.

He reached for another file, opened it and saw a picture of a bloody handprint. Stark. Deadly. A tragic story captured in one black-and-white moment. Gwen stared, too, looking intrigued when he would have expected her to be disturbed.

He closed the file. "You need to leave." *Immediately.* Because a part of him had begun to concede the possibility of her story. Which meant getting rid of the beautiful innkeeper.

"I'm not leaving you alone."

Putting the folder away, he snapped the briefcase shut and flicked the lock, hoping like hell that by tomorrow he'd remember the combination. "I'm fine. It's been a couple of hours. I'm okay." When she looked poised to argue, he frowned. "I don't want to get my memory back tomorrow and have to explain to my wife or girlfriend that I spent the night with a beautiful blonde."

"You're not married," she replied. When he raised a questioning brow, she looked away, as if embarrassed by her knowledge. "You, uh, mentioned it. Downstairs."

Right. They'd progressed at least that far during their kitchen tryst. He only hoped he wasn't a cheating SOB who'd lie about his marital state to get to a woman. But he doubted it. The very idea was offensive, and he didn't imagine his moral code would have been as affected by a bunch of pennies as his memory had been. "Thanks. But you still need to go."

"I'll just sit back down and let you go to sleep," she replied, sounding so prim he couldn't believe she was the same woman who'd been staring at his crotch a short time before. Or the one who'd kissed him when he'd threatened to kill her.

"Suit yourself," he replied with an evil smile. He reached for the waistband of his boxer-briefs. "But I sleep naked."

She visibly gulped. "How would you know?"

"My mind might not remember, but my body does. I also feel pretty sure I'll kick the covers off."

Their eyes met, hers widening as she acknowledged the

night that lay before her. Him, lying naked on the bed, uncovered, doing everything he could to make her as uncomfortable as possible. She turned to the door. "Well, your eyes are normal and your speech isn't slurred. I guess you'll be okay tonight."

He grinned, even as, for a brief second, he almost regretted forcing the issue. An hour ago, he would have thought about enticing her to stay. Now, however...well, what if it was true? What if there really was some dangerous criminal in the house? The last thing Gwen needed was to be anywhere near him.

"Promise me you'll stay in here all night," she added.

"I will." Before she could leave, he caught her arm. Her silky robe moved under his fingers, and he could feel the warmth of her skin beneath. "Good night, Gwen," he whispered, forcing himself to let her go. "And thank you. I'm not saying I believe all this...but I appreciate your concern."

She nodded once, then slipped out without another word.

Turning out the light, he stripped and got into the huge bed, wondering if he'd made a mistake. He'd pushed her away, when near him—beside, below, on top of him—was where he wanted her to be. "Enough," he growled, trying to calm his half-empty brain.

It wasn't working. Nothing could remove her image from his mind, the way the gold in her hair had reflected the light from the lamp. The way she'd smelled when he'd backed her against the wall—like sweet fruit and heady spices mixed together. The way her eyes had widened with excitement, and a hint of fear. The way she'd stared at him, with outright avarice, when his body had made it clear how much he'd wanted her. Still wanted her.

"Idiot. Think of something else."

Since sleep eluded him, and thoughts of Gwen only increased his tension, he instead tried to access some unlocked drawers within the confines of his mind. He didn't think hard, merely searching for snippets of memory, of knowledge, or intuition.

He soon found them.

Why he'd know how to make a gun out of a piece of pipe, a nail and a block of wood, he had no idea. But he knew he could do it. Which meant he probably *was* the man she claimed him to be.

"I'll be damned."

Then he remembered something else. The gun. The one in the pocket of his leather jacket, which still hung on a kitchen chair, waiting for some innocent person to stumble across it and get hurt.

"Sorry, babe, can't keep my promise," he whispered as he got up. He couldn't stay in his room, not with the chance of some kid finding the jacket, of a child's curiosity leading to tragedy.

Since his shirt and the waistband of his jeans were still damp, he merely pulled his boxer-briefs back on. As he slipped into the dark hallway, closing the door behind him, he noticed the small, handwritten sign showing the catchy name of his room. "Pretty Boy's Pad." He rolled his eyes.

Moving through the shadows felt as natural to Miles as breathing. As he headed toward the stairs, he felt much like a shadow himself. More proof. He'd done this before.

A foyer light was sufficient to guide him down the stairs and into the kitchen. The jacket was where Gwen had tossed it. A quick glance confirmed the presence of a small caliber, silver handgun in the pocket. Not knowing whether he was glad for the additional proof or not, he headed back up to his room. He'd been down and back within ninety seconds, with none the wiser. No innkeepers to panic. No terrorists to elude.

Or so he thought. Until he reached the top of the stairs, turned and saw a figure standing outside his room. He blinked hard as his vision became blurry. It *had* to be the blow to his head, or the whole Halloween atmosphere pervading the house, that suddenly made the person appear to be standing in a mist, his body emitting a strange glow, almost reflecting itself.

He squeezed his eyes shut, opening them to see that the man was still there. But he hadn't turned around, didn't seem aware of Miles's presence.

Now he knew damn well his eyes were screwed up. Because the guy down the hall didn't even seem to be standing on the floor. He looked like he was a couple of inches above it.

Get a grip, man!

Ducking into the nearest old-fashioned, recessed door frame, he tried to recall the face of the criminal he was supposedly chasing. He couldn't even try to match the photo with the man in the hall. He still didn't trust his own eyes, or his own conked brain, because the figure had looked so damned strange. Though he'd felt okay for a while now, he had to wonder if he really did have a concussion. Because he seemed to be seeing things.

Leaning out to see what the man was doing now, he was stunned to find the hall empty. The man was gone, he'd disappeared in a matter of seconds.

What the hell is this? Before he could even try to figure it out, Miles felt a cold draft of air rush past his face. It was sudden and shocking, pricking his skin as if he'd stepped out into a frigid Moscow night.

Just as quickly, almost before he'd even had time for his brain to register it, the cold pocket was gone.

"That did *not* just happen," he whispered, shaking his head in confusion. "You're imagining things."

Or maybe he wasn't. A soft, haunting laugh echoed from down the hall, as if the strange man was happy with whatever he'd done. He ducked back, close to the door, certain he was not the only one up and about in this quiet house.

Okay, Miles, think like a superspy.

All he could think was that he was a pretty pathetic secret agent. His ass was cowering in a door frame when he should be out there karate-chopping the guy straight to hell.

Or, maybe he shouldn't. Maybe he wasn't supposed to let this suspect know he was being tailed. Perhaps the case hadn't been built yet, and would be blown if he revealed himself too soon.

Dammit, if he couldn't remember his own name or birth date, how was he supposed to remember his mission? Discretion seemed the best course of action for now. So he prepared to wait the man out before slipping to the next doorway—his own room.

That was when the handwritten sign on the door where he stood caught his attention. "Pretty Boy's Pad," he whispered.

God, he really was messed up. He'd miscounted the number of doors between his room and the stairs? Not only could he not rely on his memory or mental acuity, now his eyesight was failing him.

Maybe there hadn't been a man in the hall. Or maybe there had. Either way, it was time for this supersleuth to go to bed and let his brain cells do their magic, so he could wake up in the morning and deal with the truth. Whatever that might be.

Easing into the room and shutting the door, he promptly slipped on some loose fabric on the floor. He wondered what the slippery item beneath his feet had been, but didn't care enough to turn on a lamp to see. He didn't want the man in the hall—if there really was one—noticing a light.

Though he should have been tired to the bone, he was keyed up, energetic, full of adrenaline. He somehow thought he liked this kind of espionage, maybe even got off on it. Part of him wanted to leave again, to follow the shadows, become a creature of the night, like his suspect. A wiser part told him he should go to bed and proceed tomorrow with all his circuits firing.

Stripping, he climbed into the bed, anticipating the way the cool, crisp sheets would feel against his body. But he suddenly realized three things. The sheets weren't cool. The king-size bed he'd been in minutes earlier seemed to have shrunk.

And it wasn't empty.

8

SINCE GWEN had gone to bed with Agent Miles Stone on her mind, it probably wasn't surprising that her subconscious filled her nighttime dreams with the mysterious stranger. She drifted into a light sleep, the one she always fell into moments after her weary head hit the pillow. And soon she was in that surreal place where dreams began, but consciousness hadn't fully faded.

She knew she was dreaming. But she welcomed the dream.

Miles was touching her with those big, warm hands of his. He started at her feet. Her dream lover rained alternately firm, then featherlight caresses over her ankles, and up her calves. He lingered at the back of her knee, and she arched against the sheets, wanting to sink deeper into sleep and give herself over entirely to her erotic vision.

When his mouth replaced his hands, she sighed with pleasure, able to picture his dark head against the pale skin of her thighs as he nibbled, kissed and sucked his way up her body.

"Yes," she mumbled in her sleep, still knowing she dreamed but wanting to dream on.

Miles skirted the heated place between her legs, making her crazy with want. When he pressed a heated kiss against her stomach, she writhed, tilting toward him. She wanted that intimate kiss, wanted his tongue to lick a flame of fire, to make her heated body burn even hotter. Wanted that extreme intimacy, which she'd never felt comfortable enough to share with a real lover. This phantom one, however, was most welcome to introduce her to such pleasures. She ached for him to do so.

But she couldn't control the strong-willed man, not even in her dreams. She whimpered as he teased her, made her wait, pressed kisses up her midriff, seeming to delight in sampling every inch between her navel and her collarbone. His rough cheek scraped the side of her breast and she turned toward him, wanting his mouth there. Wanting the light, teasing caresses to stop and the sensual, erotic ones to begin.

Finally she felt it. Felt a warm hand cupping her fullness, felt strong fingers tweaking her nipple into a tight bud of pure sensation. "Oh, yes."

"More?"

"Definitely," she whispered. "Taste me. Use your mouth on me, Miles. Let me feel your tongue."

He groaned. "God, you make offers I can't refuse, even though I know I should."

"Don't refuse."

Her dream Miles put his lips to her breast, sucking her nipple into his mouth. She moaned as he nibbled slightly, rolling the tip on his tongue, all the while running his hand across her belly, her hips, her thighs. But not where she wanted him most.

"Here," she murmured. "Touch me here, too." She moved her own hand down her body, not surprised her nightgown had disappeared in her dream. Reaching the curls between her legs, she slid her fingers lower, testing the slippery wetness of her body. She heard his breath grow hoarse and choppy as he watched her touch herself.

"God, you're beautiful."

"Touch me. Taste me. Show me."

His hand replaced hers. She shuddered as he dipped one finger inside her, swirling in her wetness and groaning with pleasure, obviously noting her arousal. A second finger joined the first as his thumb teasingly flicked against her clitoris, making her jerk with a pleased moan.

Gwen gradually began to realize something. She was burning up inside, but her skin was prickled from cool night air. The sheets and quilt no longer covered her and her gown really *was* gone. The mouth on her breast was not dry and dreamlike. It was hot. Moist. Agonizingly pleasurable.

She focused on the pleasure, so intense she could barely breathe, think or move. Pleasure much too intense for a dream.

Willing herself awake, she forced her eyes open and saw the impossible. Miles Stone, the man. Not the phantom.

She wasn't dreaming. This was happening. What had started out as an erotic fantasy had turned into reality.

For one wicked moment, she allowed herself to wonder at exactly which point the dream had ended. Part of her hoped he hadn't heard her beg to be tasted. Another part very much hoped he had. "Are you real?"

He smiled as he gently nipped her neck. His fingers still made her quiver as he stroked, then withdrew, swirled, then plunged in again. "Very real." His thumb moved again to her most sensitive spot, playing, tweaking, heightening sensation until she let out a long, shuddery sigh. "Are *you* real?"

More fully awake now, she nodded. "We had a conversation like this earlier tonight. About whether we were real or ghosts."

He didn't look up, continuing to kiss and suckle one

breast, then the other. His stubbled face scraped her skin with exquisite sensation. "Did we? Forgive me, I somehow don't remember."

She should have been leaping up, turning on the light, demanding answers and ordering him out. But she didn't. She didn't protest, didn't pull away, didn't consider getting up. What it came right down to was, she didn't *want* to stop. Period.

"Are we really doing this?" she asked, knowing she didn't sound shocked or dismayed. No, her voice was as lethargic as her body, made languorous by the sensations washing over her.

"Yeah. We're doing this. It's crazy, and I don't know why you changed your mind, but we're here and it's happening."

Yes. Yes, he was here. How he'd gotten into her room, she had no idea. What would happen tomorrow didn't seem to matter much, either. Because this was, indeed, what she'd wanted. She'd gone to sleep dreaming about having this man. Stranger or not, she wanted tonight with him more than she wanted to wake up tomorrow.

"I've wanted you from the minute I came to and saw you kneeling above me in the kitchen," he admitted, his voice hoarse and thick. "You're all I see when I close my eyes."

The intensity of his words turned her on almost as much as his touch. It had been a long time—perhaps forever—since she'd known a man wanted her so much. So much he'd risk anything to have her. *Anything.* "And I've wanted you from the minute I saw you standing there in the shadows."

"Tomorrow..."

"Forget about tomorrow."

The Harlequin Reader Service® — Here's how it works:

Accepting your 2 free books and gift places you under no obligation to buy anything. You may keep the books and gift and return the shipping statement marked "cancel." If you do not cancel, about a month later we'll send you 4 additional books and bill you just $3.57 each in the U.S., or $4.24 each in Canada, plus 25¢ shipping & handling per book and applicable taxes if any.* That's the complete price and — compared to cover prices of $4.25 each in the U.S. and $4.99 each in Canada — it's quite a bargain! You may cancel at any time, but if you choose to continue, every month we'll send you 4 more books, which you may either purchase at the discount price or return to us and cancel your subscription.

*Terms and prices subject to change without notice. Sales tax applicable in N.Y. Canadian residents will be charged applicable provincial taxes and GST.

If offer card is missing write to: The Harlequin Reader Service, 3010 Walden Ave., P.O. Box 1867, Buffalo, NY 14240-1867

"I think I've forgotten enough for any one lifetime," he retorted. "Tomorrow, we deal with the rest."

"And for tonight?"

He chuckled softly as he moved over her, straddling her body, his knees on either side of her hips, leaving her unable to move or resist. "Tonight," he continued, "we play."

Then he was moving lower, going down the way he'd come up earlier. But this time, he didn't slide past those most erogenous zones. No, he zeroed in on them, until his breaths tickled the swirl of soft hair shielding her mound, and his tongue flicked there, making her lose her mind.

"This is what you wanted, isn't it? To be tasted?"

Oh, God, he *had* heard. He wanted to give her exactly what she'd asked for. All she had to do was confirm that she wanted it, admit she wanted him to pleasure her in so intimate a way, and he'd do it.

Did she? She didn't have to give it another thought. *Damn right, I do.* "Yes. I want you to taste me, Miles. Then I want you to *take me.*" Remembering how much he had to give her, she almost shivered in anticipation of being filled by him. Being plunged into, over and over, while she clutched his lean hips and taut butt, letting herself be connected to him, consumed by him. Fully alive, completely a woman. For the first time in ages.

"Good."

Then his tongue moved to caress her hottest, most sensitive spot with erotic precision. That was all it took, that one hungry taste, and she came in a quick, shuddering blast of physical pleasure.

He had to have noticed. The way she cried out, Aunt Hildy probably could have noticed from downstairs. But he didn't stop, didn't take pity, didn't wait for her to come back to earth. He continued to relentlessly savor her, sucking that nub of flesh, swirling his tongue over it. Opening her legs, he draped one over his shoulder so he could gain closer access.

The kiss became more intimate, his tongue sliding lower, teasing her opening, making her crazy. She trembled, unable to believe it could be so good, so incredibly, mind-blowingly *good.*

"You shouldn't..."

"I am," he mumbled, pulling away and looking at her, completely exposed to his hungry gaze and hungrier mouth. Then, with slow deliberation, he slid his tongue inside her body, while suckling her outer folds. Her second orgasm washed over her so quickly she had no time to prepare.

"God, you're so incredibly responsive," he whispered as he moved back up until they were again face-to-face. His dark eyes glittered in the soft moonlight illuminating the room.

She'd never seen such a look of hunger on a man before. And she knew that in spite of the hour, the night was still very young. *Thank heaven.* "I've never, I mean, no one's..."

"Never?"

He stiffened, and she knew he wondered if she was a virgin. "I mean, *that* in particular. I've never done that."

His smile was decidedly masculine, cocksure. "Good. What else have you never done?"

"I'm afraid my experience is terribly limited. I've never, um...." Though the room was dark, she wondered if he could see the soft blush spreading up her body.

"What?"

"Never *reciprocated,*" she whispered. "But I want to." She wanted to taste him as he'd tasted her. Wrap her lips around that glorious erection of his and suck on him like he was a big fat lollipop. She wanted to make him as crazy with need as she'd been.

"Oh, what a wicked woman lies beneath that angelic exterior," he said, his voice low with need. "But that'll have to wait, Gwen. This is about you."

"Why me?"

"Well," he admitted, "I don't remember what I most enjoy in bed. So we'll focus on anything *you* want most."

She arched sinuously against him. "But if you don't remember what you most enjoy, maybe we should try a bit of everything and see if anything in particular rings any bells."

He chuckled softly. "Sexual smorgasbord. I like it."

So did she. The thought of a banquet of sensual experimentation with this man made her heart pound harder and her breath come faster. She wanted it all. As much as he could give. And until the morning light intruded and they had to face reality, she was going to savor every moment of the night.

"I know I'm going to love everything I get to do to you," he said, his voice husky with sensual promise. "Every time I get to do it. Now, tell me what *you* want. Tell me and we'll see how I like it, too."

Oh, boy, that was a tempting invitation. Would he think her a greedy wanton if she told him all the erotic ways she wanted to make love with him? All the positions she longed to try? The places on his body she wanted to taste and to touch?

Her previous lovers had both been meat-and-potatoes kind of guys, who hadn't seemed to even know a woman had a clitoris, much less wanted to get on a first-name basis with one. But Miles...he was a living, breathing erotic adventure waiting to be explored, to take her anywhere she wanted to go.

She suddenly felt like a kid in a candy store, not knowing what to sample first. Then she felt that thick, heavy shaft of his pressing against her legs and knew what she wanted. What she had to have. *Now.*

"Mmm," she moaned, remembering the way he'd gotten so aroused earlier tonight in his room. She'd become wet just looking at his barely contained erection. And now it was within her grasp. All she had to do was reach out and take it.

With a sultry smile, she moved her hand down his body and took him in her hand, loving the way he groaned in response.

"Greedy girl."

"Very. I want this, Miles," she said with a lingering squeeze. "And I want it now." She stroked the length of him, anticipating how good he was going to feel inside her. "Then other things...later."

"Later," he agreed.

She squeezed again, amazed at the silky smoothness of his skin, which encased such steel-hard strength. "You're not making promises you can't keep, are you?" Offering him a wicked grin, she clarified. "If tonight's all we have, I'm going to be very greedy indeed. You sure you'll be...up for it?"

He chuckled. "Sweetheart, considering I've been hard for you since the minute I set eyes on you, I don't think you have anything to worry about."

He moved between her thighs, catching her mouth in a wet kiss that tasted like heat and sex and everything she'd long been denied. Then he stiffened. "Damn, I don't have anything for protection."

Oh, God, right now she was ready to get down and kiss Aunt Hildy's toes for insisting they put condoms in the bedside tables of each of the guest rooms. Leaning over, she quickly grabbed one from the drawer and handed it to him. "We're covered."

The way he groaned with pleasure, it was as if those two words were the most seductive he'd ever heard. He sheathed himself, then nudged her thighs apart. Gwen bent her legs in welcome, arching up to meet his erection as he began to slide into her body, with a delicious restraint that left her breathless.

"Please..."

He stopped. "Please what? Stop?" He pretended to pull away.

She threw her arms around his neck and pulled him closer, a laugh on her lips. "Stop and I'll have to kill you."

He laughed softly and definitely didn't stop. He kept moving forward, closer, deeper, stretching her wide and filling her until she had to cry out with the pleasure of it. Finally, he plunged all the way into her until their bodies met from neck to toe. Gwen turned her head to cry out into her pillow, not able to contain a little cry of fulfillment.

"Good?"

She wrapped her legs around his. "Very good."

And it was. He was hot and thick, deep and strong, touching her so far inside herself she almost couldn't breathe with the intimacy of it.

Sex with a relative stranger should have felt uncomfortable, perhaps even invasive. But she'd never been more sure of one thing: pleasure like this didn't happen often. Damned if she wasn't going to grab every bit of it she could. Besides, she might not know the man too well, but Special Agent Miles Stone certainly excited her more than anyone she'd ever met. And she liked him—had liked him from the moment she'd seen him standing there in her kitchen. That was enough. For tonight, it would be enough.

"Hold on, Gwen," he whispered, his lips brushing against her temple as he ground against her in a sultry, sexual dance. "We're going for a long ride."

When he pulled out only to slide right back into her, she met his stroke, answered his moan with a cry of her own. She caressed his tight butt, her fingers digging into the strong, masculine muscles, not wanting to miss out on any part of this incredible experience. She matched his pace, and took every bit of what he offered her.

It was the most intense, incredible sex she'd ever known. Deep, fast, wet, hard. Mind-blowing.

He made no protest when she pushed him over on to his back, straddling him and doing some riding of her own. The look in his dark, glittering eyes as he watched her touch herself—cupping her own breasts as she raised then lowered herself on to his shaft over and over again—filled her with a wanton sense of feminine power that she didn't think she'd ever experienced before.

She held. She took. She clung. She thrust. She writhed. And she came so many times she nearly lost count. Finally, so did he, only to want to start all over again within minutes.

Eventually, they both slept.

HE WOKE UP when sunlight brightened the room. Not opening his eyes, he just enjoyed the warmth on his skin. And the warmth of a woman's naked body pressed against his.

Not a dream. Gwen really had come to him. She had been waiting in his bed when he'd come back upstairs during the night.

He waited for a second, to see if his memory would shift back into place with the coming of the dawn. Nothing. Considering he hadn't gotten what anyone—including the doctor—could call a good night's sleep, he supposed it wasn't too surprising.

Not that he regretted it. He didn't regret a damn thing.

"Mmm," she moaned. "It's morning already?"

"Morning comes early when you don't go to sleep until five."

They'd spent three hours indulging in the most erotic, hot and sensual sex he'd ever enjoyed. Or, at least, the most erotic, hot and sensual sex he could remember, which wasn't saying much. Still, he had a feeling last night had been one for the record books.

When a shrill piercing sound started whining from the side of the bed, he jerked. "What the hell is that?"

She stirred beside him. "My alarm clock. It's seven. I should get downstairs, the part-time cook is probably here."

He lay there, wanting to coax her into staying in bed, then thought about what she'd said. "Your alarm clock?"

She mumbled something, then reached across him, smacking at the clock. The whining stopped. "We have nine minutes."

"How would you like to spend it?" he couldn't help asking, giving her a possessive squeeze. He finally opened his eyes to see her lying sprawled on his chest.

"Unconscious."

He gave an exaggerated sigh of disappointment. "Wait a second, back to the alarm clock. You brought a clock with you from your room?"

She nodded sleepily. "I grabbed a few things. I knew I had to get up early."

So much for thinking she'd been so completely overwhelmed by desire that she'd rushed to his room and slipped into his bed in the heat of the moment. She'd brought her damn alarm clock.

"You know it's probably not a good idea for us to be seen together here." Her words were punctuated by a yawn.

"Your aunt gonna nail me with quarters this time?"

She chuckled sleepily. "Heaven forbid. I mean, since we don't know for sure if the person you're after is here, we probably shouldn't be seen leaving the same room this morning."

He hated for her to leave and tightened his arms around her, tangling his fingers in her long, blond hair. "I don't want you to go back to your room."

"Since the plumber can't come until next week, I won't be."

"Plumber? What are you talking about?"

"The one I called about the broken pipe in my room."

She'd broken a pipe in her room and called a plumber during the night? That guy had to keep some pretty late hours! "I didn't realize you had plumbing problems."

She finally rubbed a hand over her face and opened her eyes. Giving him a lethargic smile, she sat up, allowing the sheets and quilt to fall to her lap.

God, what a magnificent sight first thing in the morning. He hadn't been able to see her during the dark hours, when he'd touched, tasted, stroked and worshipped every bit of her body. Now, he drank her in visually.

She was perfectly shaped, which he'd known by touch. But he hadn't anticipated the way his body would want her all over again just at the sight of the sunlight sparkling on her hair. Not to mention the way her pretty, dark nipples grew tight under his gaze. The red marks on her neck from his mouth begged to be caressed away, as did the puffy fullness of her well-kissed lips.

"You keep looking at me that way and nobody in this house is going to get their breakfast," she murmured.

"Like I care."

She slid away, evading his hand. "I'm serious. You can't seduce me out of working. So scoot, back to your room, secret agent man, so I can go start my day."

"Back to my..."

Then he paused. The sheets and quilt tangled around Gwen's legs, and his own, were pale yellow. The ones he'd gone to bed under last night had been dark green.

He blinked and sat up straight. "What is going on here?" Mouth dropping open, he stared around the room, noting the yellow wallpaper, the white wicker furniture, the painting of ducks in a pond hanging over a fainting couch.

This wasn't the room Gwen had shown him to the night before.

This wasn't his room, period.

He froze. "How did I get here?"

She didn't make a playful joke, seeming to sense his seriousness. "Are you okay?"

He looked at her, still unable to grasp what had happened. "Gwen, I thought this was my room."

She tilted her head in confusion.

He explained. "Last night, after you left, I went downstairs to get my jacket from the kitchen, because of the gun."

"Oh, God, I'm so glad you remembered it!"

"And when I came back," he continued, "I counted the doors to go back to my room. I thought it was the next one down the hall, but the sign on this room..." He jumped out of bed and stalked to the door, pulling it open, not caring that he was naked. If somebody was walking by, too bad. "Pretty Boy's Pad," he exclaimed triumphantly.

She got up, grabbing her white bathrobe off the floor and quickly wrapping it around herself. She hurried over and peeked out into the hallway, then pushed the door closed. "What are you doing? Do you want to give some little old lady who hasn't seen a naked man in thirty years a heart attack?"

"I somehow suspect your Aunt Hildy hasn't gone thirty years without sex. She pinched my butt last night before we left the kitchen."

Gwen let out a heartfelt sigh but didn't even try to claim he'd been mistaken. Being goosed by an eighty-five-year-old wasn't easy to mistake for anything else.

"Someone else might have been passing by," she said.

"No one saw me, okay?" He pulled the door partially open again. "Read the sign."

She peeked around the edge of the door, leaning closer to read the small placard. "That doesn't make sense. This is the Bonnie Parker Boudoir. I moved up here from my regular room yesterday because of a busted pipe."

"Well, apparently when Clyde Barrow wasn't around, Bonnie hooked up with Pretty Boy Floyd," he said, thrusting a hand through his hair in complete confusion. "Somebody was messing with my head last night. I saw a person in the hall. He must have changed the signs." He didn't bother to volunteer any more details, feeling stupid enough for imagining some of the stuff he had about the guy the night before.

The color left her cheeks. "You mean you didn't intend to...you thought..."

"Yeah. I thought *you'd* slipped into *my* bed. I wasn't about to kick you out of it."

"And I thought exactly the same thing," she murmured.

Their eyes met, their stares held. Miles saw the confusion and a hint of embarrassment on her face and wondered if his expression mirrored hers.

Somehow, it hadn't seemed so crazy to accept an incredibly sensual gift from a beautiful woman during the night. What man didn't fantasize about an erotic, warm and sultry female slipping into his arms, initiating the kind of intense, incredible sex most guys only dreamed about?

But that's not what had happened.

For her to think he would have skulked into her room and gotten into her bed...what kind of guy did she imagine him to be?

He shook his head. "I should go."

He quickly grabbed his underwear and put them on, then removed the leather jacket from the chair where he'd dropped it last night. He couldn't bring himself to meet her eye. What a screwup. He couldn't even try to reassure her that he wasn't some scummy creep, the kind of man who'd deliberately sneak into a woman's bed at night and start making love to her when she wasn't even fully awake.

For all he knew, he was.

Before he could get out of the room, however, she planted herself in front of the door. "Stop right there. Let's get one thing straight."

If he hadn't been feeling so low, he'd probably get turned on by the un-Gwen-like tough attitude and tone of voice. When she put her hand flat on his chest, her fingertips sparked the same heated response they had so many times during the night.

Probably get turned on? Hell...

"I know what you're thinking."

He doubted that. And if she did, she'd probably be nervous, wondering what kind of man would be aroused—*again*—after the long night they'd had, and the truth they'd just discovered.

"You do, huh?"

"Yes. You're worried that I'm thinking you switched the signs yourself."

Not even in the ballpark. But now that she mentioned it...

"Don't," she continued. "I know you didn't. I know you're not that kind of person."

She sounded so sure, so confident of him, which was almost funny since he, himself, had no idea whether she was right or wrong. This amnesia stuff had been an annoyance at first. Now it had become a real pain in the ass. He sensed that something special could be happening between him and Gwen. But until he knew who he was, what he was like—and where he lived, for God's sake—he had no way of knowing if they could have anything more than last night. And he already felt pretty sure he wanted more.

"So, who do you suppose switched the signs on the door?" he asked, truly wondering what was going on in that beautiful head of hers. "Little green men? Your international arms dealer?"

Her face paled.

"Uh, Gwen, is there something you want to tell me?"

She looked away for a moment, her brow furrowed. When she finally met his eye again, she asked a strange question. "Is there any chance it was my Aunt Hildy you saw?" Her cheeks pinkened. "I mean, I wouldn't entirely put it past her." She blew out a frustrated sigh. "She thinks I need a man."

"Yeah, I got that impression last night," he said with a grin. Then he shook his head. "But, no, it wasn't Hildy." Though he felt almost foolish sharing the details, he admitted, "Look, I can't be sure who it was. I obviously had some blurred vision from being hit on the head. It almost looked like there was this strange light around the guy. He disappeared pretty quickly."

This time, instead of simply growing pale, she actually leaned back against the wall, then slowly sat on the chaise lounge. She finally looked up at him. "I think," she admitted, "that there are only two possible explanations."

He waited.

"Either your suspect knows you're here and was playing games with you..."

Possible. Though, if he recalled, the bad guys in James Bond flicks usually just tried to *kill* the secret agent, not mess with his head. Plus they usually did it in stupid ways, like with the help of giant sharks in tanks or killer bees or maniacs with steel teeth. Not with beautiful blondes and mixed-up bedrooms.

But this wasn't a movie and he wasn't James Bond.

"What's the other option?"

She let out an embarrassed-sounding laugh. "Or, my Aunt Hildy would say you bumped into one of her friends."

"Friends?"

"Yeah." She shook her head in bemusement. "It would probably have been Six Fingers Moe. And he's been dead for over sixty years."

9

"SO, DID YOU stay up all night fretting, or did you decide this morning that circles under the eyes are in fashion?"

Gwen knew Hildy would be commenting on her tired-looking face sooner or later today. She'd waited until after breakfast had been served and cleared away. But there was no escaping the innuendo in her question. "I'm a little tired."

Hildy gave her an expectant grin and wiggled her eyebrows. "Stayed up late making sure our unexpected guest was okay?"

Gwen nodded, ignoring the eyebrow action. "Yes, exactly." Then, lowering her voice to avoid being overheard by the cook or the part-time waitress, both of whom were busy in the kitchen, she added, "He's fine, but he didn't get his memory back yet."

Hildy didn't appear too concerned. She still had that knowing glint in her bright blue eyes and remained silent. Gwen recognized the look. Hildy had always had an unnerving way of getting people to spill their guts by simply waiting and staring, until they told all. It had worked on her as a kid more times than she could count. Whenever Hildy would come to visit Gwen and her parents, she'd manage to get all of Gwen's girlish or teenage secrets out of her within fifteen minutes of her arrival...simply by being quiet and watching.

Not this time. No way.

She busied herself putting away dishes. By the time she was finished, Hildy had helped herself to a cup of coffee—a mix of decaf and regular that Hildy called unleaded with a slug—and was sitting at a table in the empty dining room. Still staring. Still smiling. Patient as ever.

Deciding the best defense was a good offense, Gwen asked, "Did you sleep all right?"

Hildy shrugged, not saying a word.

"No more problems with your hip?"

Another shrug.

"The guests seemed to like breakfast."

Hildy merely smiled a little more, her sweet face masking what Gwen knew to be an incredibly sharp, strong-willed mind.

But Gwen had a secret weapon. There was one surefire way to get the elderly woman to talk. Giving Hildy a nonchalant glance as she idly checked their supply of linen napkins in the sideboard, she asked, "How'd those bran muffins do yesterday?"

Bingo. Eighty-five-year-olds loved talking about their digestive systems. For five minutes, Hildy reiterated the importance of fiber and her certainty that she would have died years ago had it not been for the magic of Metamucil. Then her voice trailed off and she frowned. "You did that on purpose."

Gwen grinned, kissed the old woman's temple and brushed a strand of fine white hair off her face. She sat next to her aunt, sipping from her own cup of strong coffee. "Yep."

"I want the dirt."

"There is no dirt. Mr. Stone is safe in his room. I brought him up some breakfast a few minutes ago." He'd been in the shower, which was just as well. She sensed he could easily distract her. Sensed? Heck, she knew that for a fact.

When they'd first parted this morning, she'd asked him to stay in his room until the doctor could examine him again. In truth, she didn't want him wandering the house, running into someone he might not know—but who might know him. As it was, it hadn't mattered much. The mysterious foreign gentleman had not emerged from his third-floor room, missing the morning meal altogether.

He wasn't the only one. Mick Winchester hadn't shown up, either. Her first impulse was to believe Mick was sleuthing or doing whatever it was a "contact" to the feds did. Then, when Dr. Wilson hadn't come down, she'd rethought her conclusion. She'd lay ten to one odds that if she knocked on the door to the Lady in Red Room, Mick would answer. She suspected she and Miles Stone hadn't been the only strangers getting friendly last night.

Just thinking about Miles, about seeing him again soon, made her pulse speed up. Yes, she'd sensed his withdrawal when he'd realized what had happened with their room signs. Gwen wondered why she didn't feel the same way—why the morning hadn't brought a sense of unease or embarrassment. It hadn't, though. Whatever the reason, however he'd ended up in her bed, she was glad it had happened. Last night was something she'd never forget, or regret.

Even if it *had* ended with him staring at her like she was crazy for suggesting he'd seen a ghost during the night.

He'd thought she was kidding. She hadn't corrected his assumption. Heck, she didn't really believe it herself. But stranger things had certainly happened in this house.

Part of her eagerly anticipated slipping away to his room this morning to continue their discussion. Another part was jittery as a cat about facing a man who'd touched her in places she didn't know it was legal to be touched...or that it would feel so darn good. She sighed at the memory, unable to help it, even though it added fuel to her Aunt Hildy's inquisitive fire.

"So, did you and Mr. Stone get to chat a while last night?"

"Uh-huh."

"I don't suppose he remembered whether or not he's married? Or if he's a psycho killer just posing as a spy or anything, hmm?"

She laughed softly. "He's not married—we cleared that up before you conked him. And I'm certainly not afraid of him."

"You're sure he's not a button man on the lam?"

Gwen couldn't recall what that meant. But knowing Hildy, she almost certainly wasn't referring to a minister on a mission of mercy or anything closely resembling one. "Pretty sure."

Hildy had such a streak of danger-love running through her blood that she looked for it wherever she thought she might find some. That trait hadn't served her well in her younger years, when she'd run away from her wealthy Boston family at the age of fifteen and become the girlfriend of a petty thief. She might have gotten bored and come home if that petty thief hadn't been the cousin of one of Johnnie Dillinger's gang members.

Today, not many people remembered the details of the charming bank robber and his creative partners in crime. But Gwen knew the stories. She'd sat at Hildy's knee absorbing them as a kid, the gorier and more dangerous the better.

Though things had changed—*Gwen* had changed—

Hildy still, on occasion, talked about her past. The family had kept their secret well, so the only one she had to talk to was her niece. Most of the stories still intrigued Gwen. But the idea that her aunt had been at the *real* Little Bohemia Inn a mere hour before the infamous Dillinger shootout of April, 1934, always made her shiver.

That was another reason Gwen had tried to dissuade Hildy from this gangster inn idea, considering the elderly woman's fragile mental state. The doctors believed Hildy was strong enough to embrace that part of her past and that Gwen should let her. So far, Hildy had enjoyed the chance to blend her teen years with her golden ones, never getting the two mixed up in her mind. And she'd finally found a place where she seemed at home. Ghosts and all. Gwen had never seen her aunt as happy as she'd been since they'd moved here last year. Which made it all worthwhile.

"You do look tired," Hildy said after the two of them shared a moment of silence. Then she added, "Yet there's a sparkle in your eye that I haven't seen in a long time." The old woman didn't sound inquisitive, or titillated. Instead, she looked at Gwen with an expression of genuine love. That look told Gwen—more than words might have—how worried Hildy had been about her.

"I've been rather unpleasant to be around, haven't I?"

Hildy shook her head. "No, honey-cakes. Not unpleasant. Just so darned unhappy."

"I'm not unhappy." She liked her new life, liked Derryville, liked her home and the friends she'd made.

"That was the wrong word," Hildy admitted with a frown. "You've been...spiritless. Unadventurous. Taking life as it comes instead of taking it by the..."

"I get the picture," Gwen interrupted with a soft laugh. "Which doesn't endear you to a person, does it?"

Hildy shook her head in disgust. "No, it doesn't."

"Aunt Hildy, maybe I don't want a life of intrigue, danger and adventure." But even as she said the words, she questioned them. The past twenty-four hours had been among the most exciting of her life. Meeting Miles, getting caught up in the danger and the thrill...and, oh Lord, the passion. She couldn't remember when she'd felt more alive.

She knew it couldn't last. A future with the dashing spy was completely impossible. But, for once, she was going to take what she could get for as long as she could have it. Somehow, being certain they had no tomorrow was giving her the strength to run full tilt into a wild, sensual adventure today. It was as if by already preparing for the moment he left, she could enjoy the time she had. Half-trying to convince herself, she added, "Excitement's fine, but there's something to be said for a quiet, safe existence."

Hildy pursed her lips. "A quiet, safe existence. Like the one your parents lived." Her voice shook as she added, "That was supposed to enable them to grow old together, wasn't it?"

Gwen knew what Hildy meant. The moisture in her fine old eyes and the audible catch in her voice said more than her words ever could. Hildy had truly loved her only nephew—Gwen's dad. And she'd loved Gwen's mother, too. Hildy had been every bit as crushed by their untimely death as Gwen.

Gwen's parents had been the epitome of safe, conservative Boston traditionalists. Loving, quiet, restrained. They'd been surprised by Gwen's arrival, their "change of life baby" they'd called her. But they'd never made her feel unwanted in any way.

They should never have died because of something as foolish as a buckled railroad tie and a high-speed derailment. Now, she was able to acknowledge that a part of her had died with them that day two years ago. Without a doubt, it had been the part that had been most like Great-aunt Hildy.

"Point taken," she murmured.

"What I'm saying, sugar lips," Hildy continued, "is that you don't have to live dangerously to find excitement in this world. And living carefully and quietly isn't a guarantee of safety and happiness." Hildy glanced out the window, obviously lost in thought. "A person can find thrills in a regular day-to-day life. It doesn't always have to be about physical danger. Taking an emotional risk can sometimes be much more potent."

Gwen knew what she meant. She was even able to admit that Aunt Hildy was right. Gwen had not allowed herself to take an emotional risk in a long time...not since her engagement. Even then, part of her had always known she hadn't given her whole heart away to her ex-fiancé.

So, truthfully, the biggest risk she'd taken in years had happened right in this house. *Last night.* Whew, when she got back into the risk-taking game, she got back in with a vengeance.

"Of course, there's something to be said for physical risks." The older woman grinned as she shook her head in disbelief, still gazing at something in the backyard. "Sometimes they can be just plain fun." She glanced at Gwen, then tilted her head toward the window, silently ordering her to look out. "Nothing like rescuing a honey of a man dangling from a third-floor ledge to get the blood pumping."

Not sure what Hildy was talking about, and almost afraid to find out, Gwen followed her stare. Seeing a flash of something black against the light gray paint on the side of the house, she leaped to her feet and hurried to the window. The dining room was in the middle of the horseshoe-shaped building, and she had an unobstructed view of both wings of the house. All was normal on the east side. But on the west...

Her jaw dropped. "Good God!"

A black-clad figure dangled off a third-story window ledge. She recognized him easily, particularly since those taut legs had been tangled with hers a few hours before. Her fingers still tingled from holding tight to that gorgeous hard body of his.

A gorgeous hard body that now hung perilously a good twenty-five feet or so above the ground.

Miles Stone.

"OKAY, GENIUS, mental note. Not a great idea to try climbing up the side of a building without knowing whether or not you have a problem with heights."

He kept a tight grip on the decorative, wrought-iron grate covering the third-story window, willing himself not to look down. Looking down meant acknowledging just how frigging high up he was. Staring straight ahead—counting the miniscule cracks in the gray wood siding—kept him focused and able to pretend he was dangling only two feet above the ground. Not two dozen.

"All you have to do is swing left, back into the tree," he told himself yet again. Easier said than done. The branch he'd climbed over on was now *above* him—he'd had to bend low to grab the grating. It'd mean a leap to try to reach it. Or else he could jump down and try to land on one that was farther away.

Jeez, it had seemed so simple. Someone had slipped a note under his door, saying the man he was seeking was staying in the room directly above his. It said to be discreet about his investigation, and that his contact would meet him in the gardener's shed at noon.

He'd planned to stay put, in his room, trying to relax his brain enough to get some sleep and to get his memories back. But the note had filled him with adrenaline. He could no more just stay quiet, waiting for Gwen to return with his breakfast, than he could have stopped himself from making love to her the previous night. Some situations demanded action, not thought.

Right now, however, thought wasn't sounding so bad.

"Moron. You couldn't just stick to the stairs, wait the suspect out, then sneak in after he'd left," he muttered.

He'd tried that option first. But since he had heard the man moving around behind his closed door, he'd crept back downstairs and formulated another plan. The huge oak tree right outside his window extended almost to the roof of the house. It had seemed like such a simple thing—climb out on one limb, go up a few yards, get in close to the window to see what the perp was doing. Wait for him to leave, then jimmy the window lock, climb in and snoop.

The plan had worked well at first. He'd hugged the tree as he'd scaled it. Focused only on the third-floor window, he'd spent a few minutes watching the portly, nearly bald gentleman typing away on a laptop computer. He ached to get at that computer, to check the files, run through the hard drive for any incriminating data.

When the man had left, closing his door behind him, Miles had made his move. Climbing up one more branch, he'd maneuvered over and lowered himself to the window ledge.

Then he'd looked down.

Bi-i-i-g mistake. Huge. *Gigantic* mistake. Error of epic proportions here.

Overwhelmed by the spinning sensation of vertigo, he'd lost his concentration. His foot had slipped off the ledge, and he'd barely managed to catch himself on the grating. Luckily, it appeared he worked out in his real life—his arms were strong. They had to be, because he was probably going to be hanging here for hours, until he figured out what the hell he was going to do.

After a minute or two, he'd thought to feel around with his feet and found a bit of a toehold on the ledge above the window below. That relieved some of the pressure on his arms, but it sure didn't get him out of his predicament.

So, here he hung, frozen like an ancient statue, waiting to fall or get caught. He hadn't decided which he preferred when he heard a screech of metal from below.

"Miles, hold on!"

Like he had a choice?

"I'm coming."

He recognized the voice. Hmm...if he wasn't mistaken, Gwen Compton had said something very much along those lines, though under different circumstances, just a few hours ago. In her bed.

He much preferred that connotation of the sentence.

Turning his head, he watched as the end of a metal extension ladder came into view, right beside his shoulders. Something whizzed through his brain, a mostly faded image of a disappearing ladder, but the thought was gone before he could grab it.

"Okay, I'm holding the ladder steady. All you have to do is swing on to it," she said from below, her voice a loud whisper that cut through the silence of the morning.

"It appears I don't care for heights," he replied, taking deep, even breaths.

"You said something about that last night."

"Thanks for mentioning it." After a brief pause, he heard a squeak of metal and knew she was on the ladder. "Gwen, *don't*."

She didn't respond.

"I mean it, don't climb up here!"

Within just a few seconds, he looked over and saw the top of her head, not far from his thigh.

"Too late. I did," she said. "Now, all you have to do is move your leg over and I'll make sure you plant it directly on the rung. Then we'll ease back down together, okay?"

"Gwen," he bit out, "who's holding the damn ladder?"

She flushed. Before he could warn her not to look down, her head turned, her eyes shifted. And she turned to stone.

"Shit," he muttered, recognizing the deer-in-the-headlights look on her face. It probably matched his own. "Now we're both stuck."

They stayed that way for a full minute... Gwen looking down, him watching her. Finally, she lifted her eyes as she tightened her arms around the metal extension ladder in a death grip. "Uh, Miles, have any bright ideas?"

"I was going to suggest that you go through the house, come up to this room, open that window and give me your hand."

She nibbled her lip. "I guess that won't work now."

"Guess not."

Smiling, she said, "My Aunt Hildy knows where we are."

"Oh, great. Perfect. We'll have the eighty-five-year-old up here with us in a minute. Maybe she'll bring a few guests along—breakfast on the roof, anyone?"

Her smile faded. "Okay, nix the idea of Hildy helping us." Then she shot him an accusing look. "You're a secret agent, aren't you supposed to have emergency gear for any contingency? James Bond always did."

He raised a brow. "What do you expect? A helicopter in my hat, a parachute under my trench coat?"

In spite of the perilous situation, she grinned. "That's Inspector Gadget, not James Bond." Her grin turned into a giggle, then a laugh. "I was talking about a rope or something."

Miles was unable to resist her bright smile, the way the sunshine caught the gold in her long braid and turned her eyes into pure, molten amber. Those beautiful eyes were wide, still showing a hint of fear, but now also sparkling with excitement.

He finally began to laugh, too. "No rope. And since I'm not wearing a hat or a trench coat, there's no helicopter or parachute, either. Any other ideas, bright eyes? My arms are getting tired."

She shifted her gaze, staring at his arms and his straining shoulders, then she licked her lips in a blatantly appreciative reaction. "I figured you must work out. Now I'm sure of it." Her voice sounded decidedly reminiscent.

"Stop staring at me like that."

"Like what?" she asked, all innocence.

"Like you want to gobble me up."

"I do."

He shook his head as a rush of heat descended from his brain to his groin. "Do you know how difficult it is to hold on here? The last thing I need is a hard-on pushing me that much farther away from the damn wall."

Her laughter rang out, echoing in the quiet, partially enclosed corner of the house. Then she got serious. "Well, if I remember correctly," she lowered her gaze to stare at his hips, "And I *do*..." She wagged her eyebrows suggestively. "You *are* in danger of being pushed a lo-o-o-ng way from the wall."

"Knock it off," he said with a husky laugh. "I need to concentrate."

"Concentrate on what?" she asked, her voice still dreamy, as if she'd forgotten where they were, what was happening, and could only think of the intimacies they'd shared in her bed the night before. He was having difficulty not focusing on the same things.

"Concentrate on what I'm going to do to you after we get down from here."

"What's that?" Her question held a note of suggestiveness that hinted at what she'd like him to do.

"First I'm gonna spank you for putting yourself in danger."

Her eyes widened.

"Then I'm going to make love to you until you don't have the energy to get yourself into any more trouble."

"Look who's talking about getting into trouble."

"Touché."

"But I do like the second part of the plan." Then she gave him the kind of warm look that could turn any man into a drooling moron. "Is it crazy for me to say I'm *so* glad I met you, Miles Stone?"

He shook his head. "It somehow makes sense to me."

"I can't remember when I've had a better time."

"You don't get out much, do you?"

She chuckled.

"Okay," he said, realizing that during their short conversation, he'd somehow gained some calm and was able to assess the situation rationally. As long as he didn't look down again, he might be all right and be able to get them both out of this mess. "I'm going to try to pull myself up onto the ledge and see if I can get the window open."

She looked nervous, watching with wide eyes and practically chewing a hole in her lip. It took a little effort, and some luck in finding additional footholds for his toes, but he was able to do it. Once he'd pulled himself to a standing position on the thin ledge, he unfastened the grate, stepping aside to ease it open.

Holding his breath, he pushed on the window. It moved. Thank God the criminal was the trusting sort. "We're set."

Within a minute, the two of them were standing in the empty room. As soon as her feet hit the floor, Gwen threw her arms around his neck. "Thank you. I'll never get on a ladder again."

"You're just saying that to get out of the spanking."

She leaned close, nibbling on his earlobe and blowing lightly on his neck. "Maybe I'd like it...."

Naughty girl. Judging by her tone of voice, and the pounding of her heart which he could feel against his own chest, she was every bit as keyed up, as turned on and charged with adrenaline as he was. God, what a rush.

"So where do we start?" she asked, stepping away from him to look around the room. "I saw Mr. Mysterious coming downstairs as I was racing to get the ladder to save you."

He crossed his arms, raising a brow. "Who saved whom?"

She blew out an impatient breath. "Details, details. Come on, what do we have to do? Toss the room? Plant a bug?"

He didn't know precisely what she was talking about. Come to think of it, he really had *no* idea what he was supposed to do. Getting into the room had been the objective.

He hadn't thought much beyond that. Then he spied the computer. "I want to check out his hard drive. I saw him typing while I was in the tree."

"Good plan. You do that, I'll search his stuff."

It was the thrill in her voice that really made him stop and watch her. Gwen positively sparkled. Gone was the quiet, reserved woman who'd tried to resist telling him the truth last night. The innkeeper had not merely dropped her self-protective shell, she'd erupted out of it and gone full tilt into an adventure.

He liked that about her. Hell, he liked *everything* about her. For a second, he wondered if he were an emotionally impulsive kind of guy in his real life, because, as crazy as it sounded considering they'd only known each other a day, he could very easily picture being in love with this woman. "Gwen?"

She looked over as she reached for the door to the closet.

"Whatever happens when I get my memory back..." He paused, unsure how to say what he was feeling. Asking her to stick around, to see if they might have a shot at something permanent, seemed awfully dangerous considering he didn't even know where he lived. Or if he had a terminal disease or something.

"Yes?"

Before he could continue, he heard something that made him freeze. Voices. In the hall. Right outside the door.

They were about to be caught red-handed.

10

"SOMEBODY'S COMING."

Her eyes widened in shock as they both began to look for an escape route. Miles glanced at the window, quickly nixing the idea of going down the way they'd come up. He'd almost rather get caught than try to get the two of them back to the ground without breaking their necks.

"It's him," Gwen whispered. She stood closer to the door and was listening intently to the voices of the people speaking in the hall. "And a woman. It might be his buyer, Miss Jones."

Miles had glanced through the dossier on his suspect that morning, so he immediately knew whom she meant.

"No, wait, it's Jenny, the part-time housemaid. He's asking if a tray can be brought up to his room." She frowned, fisted a hand and put it on her hip. "You wouldn't need a tray, mister, if you'd come down for breakfast on time. What a waste of a good soufflé. We're going to have to rethink that entrée if guests are going to ignore seating times. It goes flat after an hour."

He didn't know whether to laugh or groan. She was kvetching over the manners of a rude houseguest when they were about to get busted by an internationally known criminal. "Gwen!"

She finally seemed to remember their situation. "Come on."

Darting toward him on sneaker-clad feet, she took his

hand and tugged him toward the large, walk-in closet. She shut the wooden door behind them. He heard the suspect enter the bedroom less than ten seconds later.

They remained silent, barely breathing, hardly able to see each other in the darkness. His heart pounded wildly in his chest. Embarrassment could be the least of their problems. They could be in real danger.

And yet, right now, as crazy as it seemed, he wanted to kiss her even more than he wanted not to get caught.

He couldn't resist. Reaching out in the dark, he grabbed her shoulders and tugged her into his arms, finding her mouth and catching it in a hot, wet kiss. She kissed back, just as frenzied, driven by adrenaline and excitement, writhing against his body and emitting a soft groan when she felt his physical response. "He'll find us. This is crazy," she finally whispered when they parted to suck in a few deep, ragged breaths.

"I know."

Then she grabbed his hair and pulled him down for another kiss. Their tongues met and danced, tasting, sucking, getting deeper, closer. He cupped her face, tangling his fingers in her hair, loosening her braid. Her hands moved down to encircle his hips. She lifted one leg, hooking it behind his and bringing their lower bodies into direct contact. He gave a soft, guttural groan, wanting nothing more than to drive into her, to lose himself in her body as he had the night before.

They might have done it right there. He was that far gone, that aroused, that high on danger and intrigue and her taste and her smell. Miles was one second from unzipping his pants and taking her up against the wall of the closet when they heard the man in the bedroom begin to speak.

They instantly pulled apart. "Someone else is in there," she said in a ragged whisper as she sucked in audible breaths.

He struggled to hear over the pounding of his own charged blood in his veins. "I don't hear anyone else."

"Then who's he talking to?"

"No idea," he replied, his voice as quiet as hers. "Is there a phone in the room?"

"We haven't had time to rewire the whole house. This used to be the servants quarters and there was no extension up here."

So, who was the criminal talking to in that low tone of voice? Was he speaking into a cell phone? Unable to resist, he leaned closer, easing the door open a crack, cursing the slight squeak that was magnified by the tiny space and his own desire for silence.

The balding man didn't appear to hear it. He sat at the desk, speaking into a tiny microcassette recorder. Miles sighed in relief, grateful they were still dealing with just the one suspect. "He's talking to himself."

As he watched, the man turned the recorder off and placed it on the desk. He fiddled with the few strands of hair on his head for a moment, patting them into place as precisely as any beauty queen. After he had that settled to his satisfaction, he lay down on the four-poster, antique bed, kicking off his shoes and letting them clunk to the floor.

"Hell, we're stuck. He's on the bed, taking a nap. There's no way he won't hear us trying to leave," Miles whispered.

"I just realized something. There's another way. Follow me."

He could barely make out her silhouette in the dark

closet, but felt her moving past him toward the back wall. Then a crack of light appeared.

"It's a small, secondary access panel into the attic," she explained.

Left with no other choice, he followed.

THEIR REFUGE wasn't a bad hiding place. It was definitely better than the alternative—being caught. They were safely sheltered, well hidden, warm and dry. Not dangling from a building, at least.

Yes, things could be much worse. Which was good, considering they'd be stuck in the dusty attic of the Little Bohemie Inn for a while. Gwen had barely been able to congratulate herself on getting them out of the suspect's closet when she'd realized they weren't free and clear yet. Because of the way the house had been renovated to make two large suites out of the upstairs quarters, the large, main access door into the attic now led down a few steps into another room. An *occupied* room. So they had to stay put.

She could have been doing any one of a dozen chores. Instructing the maid, discussing the menu with the cook, making sure the rooms were tidied and beds made, that the guests were happy and had everything they needed. She had calls to make, bills to pay, repairs to oversee and visitors to entertain. All the things expected of an innkeeper. None of which she was going to be able to accomplish. Instead she was trapped inside a cavernous room filled with old furniture, trunks, boxes, dressmaker's dummies and piles of old newspapers.

The sun provided sufficient light through the slatted vents on either side of the house, and from under the eaves. Yet it wasn't so bright that all the shadows were chased away. The recesses of the room remained draped in darkness, dust and cobwebs. Adrenaline still pounded in her blood after their close call, making her jumpy, to the point where she half expected some ghostly figure to emerge from one of the darkened corners of the room.

The innkeeper, however, couldn't muster up much disappointment at her situation. Because, oh, lordy, the company was to die for.

"What time is it?" he asked.

She glanced at her watch. "Almost noon."

"I think I'm going to miss my appointment with my mysterious contact. He wanted to meet me in the gardener's shed at noon."

She frowned. "We don't have a gardener's shed anymore. We tore it down after we moved in."

Miles ran his hand through his hair in visible frustration. "Guess this real-estate guy's not too good at the spy game." Then he glanced toward the closed access door. "What time do you think most guests will leave for lunch? I figure one or both rooms will empty if people start leaving the inn."

"Maybe an hour. I'm thankful the elderly couple in the other room were talking, not, uh...being amorous, when we peeked."

He cringed, obviously as glad as she that they hadn't peered through the second door to see two ninety-year-old self-claimed former movie stars doing the nasty. "You're not kidding. That would be one memory I'd happily forget."

"You told me last night that they're counterfeiters."

He sighed, shaking his head. "We're surrounded by suspects in this place, aren't we?"

They spoke in subdued tones, confident they could evade discovery, but not wanting to risk being overheard. Then again, if they were, the guests at the inn would probably enjoy thinking they'd heard the voices of a pair of ghost lovers whispering in the attic of the Little Bohemie.

"Anyone else I should be worried about? Your aunt's ghost friends, do they hang around up here, too?" he asked.

She wondered for a second if he'd been read her thoughts. He was likely humoring her. Hadn't she been doing the same thing with Hildy for the past ten months? Still, sometimes she did wonder... "No, they live in the basement. Besides, it's Saturday morning. They're likely with Hildy, watching cartoons."

"Cartoons." His tone was laced with amused disbelief.

"Yep. Moe likes Nickelodeon, mainly because of the name. I guess he remembers the real nickel movie machines from his childhood or something."

His shoulders shook as he laughed. "Moe. He's the one with six fingers on one hand, right?"

"No." She raised a curious brow. "Why would you think that?"

"Well, didn't you call him Six Fingers Moe?"

"Oh...gotcha. No, he doesn't have six fingers on one hand. He has five on one and just his pinky on the other."

He winced. "That have anything to do with the way he died?"

She shook her head. Hildy had told her this story with relish during her childhood years, so she explained matter-of-factly. "He was apparently a bit sticky-fingered. Scarface didn't like the way he lifted a pack of cigarettes after a board meeting at some Chicago hotel one time. So he taught him a lesson."

"Scarface. Capone. Riiiight," he replied, amused, apparently having no idea she was speaking the truth.

Gwen didn't take offense at his skepticism. She, herself,

didn't entirely believe in the ghost of Six Fingers Moe. Or the two other ghosts—Mackey the Fish and Lou Bones—who, Hildy said, sometimes popped in for a gab. But the people themselves, at least, had once existed. Hildy still had pictures of herself with all three of them. Gwen had been particularly interested in the pictures of Moe Marcini, who'd definitely had only six fingers.

Miles walked around exploring the room, picking up a hatbox here or an old newspaper there. He seemed fascinated by the collection of junk and antiques. Gwen understood. She'd felt the same way the first time she'd been in this place. Not dismayed or disturbed by the clutter, rather she'd been filled with curiosity over the history of those who had touched these things, sat in these chairs, worn these clothes. She still wondered about it.

Built to 1800s standards, the attic could really have been considered another room and was perfect for storage. It was fully floored, with beamed ceilings and a huge ventilation fan, which had probably been installed long after the house was built. The attic extended the entire front of the house, from the east wing to the west, and had probably once upon a time provided a wonderful hide-and-seek spot for any children who'd lived in the place.

One thing was certain, Fat Lip Nathan had needed every bit of the space. The man had been a saver.

"Fascinating." Miles finally sat on an old chaise lounge, one of the pieces of furniture Gwen and Hildy had stashed up here after taking possession of the house. "There's so much interesting stuff up here."

"Definitely," she replied. "I haven't had time to explore all the trunks. From what I've seen, there are clothes, journals, photo albums and newspapers going back decades. Plus, of course, all the furniture."

After they'd heard from Nathaniel Marsden's lawyer, and come to explore Hildy's unexpected inheritance, Gwen had been surprised by the quality of furniture in the gothic-looking old place. The dingy exterior of the home had done a good job of discouraging visitors, and concealing the wealth—and likely, the criminal past—of its owner. Inside, there'd been a ton of beautiful antiques that would have made any Boston dealer drool.

Most of the pieces had been in good condition, others just in need of refinishing. That particular project had been perfect for Gwen last spring. There was something calming about bringing lovely old pieces back to life, working with her hands, uncovering a beautiful oak finish from beneath years' worth of varnish, paint and neglect.

It had been during those spring days in the workshop that she'd healed from the hurt of her broken engagement. She'd come to love her new life, and to accept the loss of the one she'd left in Boston.

"This chair's not bad. Just needs new upholstery," Miles said. "Did you bring *any* of this with you when you moved in?"

She shook her head. "Everything came with the house. These are the pieces we didn't need for the B & B."

The attic also contained other stored remnants of the former owner. The first thing Hildy had wanted to do was check the oversized trunks for any weapons, body parts, jewelry or stolen money. She'd seemed almost disappointed to have found nothing more than dusty dishes, papers, linens and old clothes. Though she'd never have admitted it to Hildy, Gwen had been a little disappointed, too.

One stack of old black-and-white photos had made Aunt Hildy cry. She'd hidden the pictures and refused to let Gwen see them.

"So," he asked as he reclined on the chaise, dropping his feet to either side and patting the end for her to sit down, "how'd you end up an inn owner?"

She sat. "Aunt Hildy inherited the house from someone she...grew up with." She carefully explained how they'd come to be here, leaving out key details. Like anything that involved too much of Hildy's past.

He must have heard something in her voice, some hint of strain when she talked about moving here from back east. "Why were you so anxious to get out of Boston? Sounds like you had a great job. And I find it hard to believe there was no one special who didn't want you to stay."

She gave a humorless laugh. "A few months earlier and there would have been."

"Tell me," he ordered softly.

So she did. She told him about her relationship with Rick, spilling out the whole sorry story of her broken engagement in a subdued whisper. At one point she stood up and paced the room. Yes, she wanted him to hear the truth, especially since they'd become involved. That didn't mean she wanted to watch his face while she told him. Especially knowing he could hear the faint vestige of hurt she couldn't completely hide.

Not that she was really hurting—even before meeting Miles, she'd recognized how much happier she was now than she'd ever been in Boston. Still, she hadn't talked to anyone about the whole situation since the day after she'd canceled her wedding.

"So, not only was he cheating on you, he'd been stealing information from your office and using you to find out what he could about your boss? All for his own benefit?"

"Yep. Pretty sordid, huh? Hildy was the only one who'd seen through him."

"You haven't said anything about other family members. Your parents?"

"They were killed in that big train derailment outside Washington, D.C., two years ago."

"I'm sorry," he murmured.

She nodded her thanks for his words of consolation, and the tender look that accompanied them. "It certainly made me think about things. What I wanted, what I would do with my life." *What risks I'd take.*

"Did you have any other family?"

Shaking her head, she replied, "It's just been me and Hildy for a long time."

"Until Rick the prick."

She chuckled. "Right. And as you can tell, the man I was going to marry turned out to be someone I never really knew at all." She shivered lightly, though the attic wasn't too cold.

Holding out a hand, he pulled her back down, not letting her sit at the end of the chaise, but tugging her on to his lap. He wrapped his arms around her, offering warmth, comfort, understanding. "I think you had it backwards, Gwen. I think the truth is, the SOB never knew *you.*"

Unsure what he meant, she raised a brow.

"He thought he'd found a serene, unemotional woman who'd accept a marriage with no passion and wouldn't put up too much of a fuss if she found out how cutthroat and ambitious he was."

Her jaw dropped open. Maybe the man really was a mind reader. Because the physical side of her relationship with Rick had, indeed, been their one big problem area. No passion pretty much summed it up. "How'd you figure that out?"

He replied with a wolfish grin. "I might have lost my

memory, but I definitely remember the way you responded last night." He shifted her in his lap, but not before she felt him hardening beneath her bottom. "And some of the things you said about what you *hadn't* done before."

Heat stained her cheeks as she acknowledged what he meant. Lordy, there may have been things she hadn't tried before, but they'd hit quite a lot of them during the previous night.

He seemed to sense her sudden embarrassment because he stopped teasing her. "Maybe he was looking for a trophy wife, a beautiful, sedate woman to host his parties, but one who'd look the other way while he fooled around on the side," he said. "And one who'd like the money enough not to turn him in."

"You might be right." Her words sounded breathy to her. All she could focus on was their proximity, the way his skin smelled, the way his warm breath felt as he whispered. She wiggled again, intentionally upping the tension, almost sighing with pleasure when she felt the erection he couldn't disguise.

"He didn't know you. He didn't know the Gwen I made love to last night." He laughed softly, taking her braid and gently plucking bits of cobweb and what looked like a fleck of gray house paint from it. "He *definitely* didn't know the Gwen who climbed up that ladder, came through that window, and dragged me into the closet." He leaned close and kissed her neck. "The one who's intentionally driving me crazy with her sweet butt and innocent little sigh."

She nibbled her lip. "I'm not sure this is the real Gwen, either."

He pulled away to stare at her, silently challenging her to think about it, to face herself, who she was and what she wanted. Finally, slowly, she began to smile, acknowledging a truth she'd been denying for a long time. "Okay, maybe it is. I guess I never realized just how much of myself I'd buried after my parents died. Rick just threw in the last few shovelsful."

His expression was triumphant. He ran his fingers across her jaw, touching her ear, then the pulse in her neck. "I'm crazy about you no matter who you are. I wouldn't have you any other way," he said in a husky whisper.

"With you, I remember how much I like being daring," she admitted, almost surprising herself with the realization. "I used to like to be wild. Living in that heart-pounding place between risky and downright perilous. Growing up, I wanted all of that, wanted to be just like Hildy, to have passion and excitement and danger be a part of my everyday vocabulary." She stared at him, growing serious. "You gave that back to me, Miles. I wasn't kidding when I said this has been the best time I've ever had. I somehow think I've been waiting to meet someone like you, so I could remember a part of myself I'd let slip away."

Though she'd never felt more self-aware, more certain, she couldn't stop another shiver at one inescapable realization. This amazing man, who'd awakened needs within her that had long lain dormant, who'd reopened a part of herself she hadn't realized had been closed off, still didn't know for sure who he was.

But Gwen knew. He was the wild, adventurous spirit she'd been unconsciously seeking her whole adult life.

"You cold?" he whispered, obviously having felt her shiver.

She shook her head, thrusting away the remnants of doubt. "I'm fine, it's not that cold up here. Are you cold?"

He nodded gravely.

"Do you want me to dig through the trunks and find something to put on us?"

"I only want one thing on me." He pulled the elastic off the end of her braid and sifted the long strands of hair between his fingers. *"You."*

Miles ran the tip of his finger across her shoulder, trailing her collarbone, gently touching the hollow of her throat. They he moved his hand lower. Lower. Until his fingertips rested at the button of her jeans. "And there's only one way I want to warm up."

Her heart skipped a beat as she went soft and warm, deep inside, from just the simple touch of his fingers. "Oh? How's that?"

"With body heat."

"Works for me," she said, her voice nearly a purr.

He unsnapped, then unzipped her jeans. Tugging her thin sweater loose from her waist, he began pushing it up. The cool air in the attic brought goose bumps to her chest, but her shiver wasn't caused by anything cold. No, it was pure heat that had her nearly shaking. The heat of his stare, of his hands, of his breath. The way his fingertips brushed the skin of her belly, then her ribs as he tugged the sweater off. Then it was gone, and he began to toy with the straps of her lacy bra.

"Mmm," she moaned, wanting more than just that soft, delicate brush of his fingers.

He complied, pushing the lace away, lowering the straps down her arms to release her breasts. "I think I'm going to like making love to you in the daytime," he muttered hoarsely, his eyes studying every inch of her. "I couldn't see you well enough last night."

She wanted him to see her. Wanted to drink in that expression of pure, male appreciation on his face. Unfastening her bra, she tossed it to the floor and moved closer, straddling his thighs. He groaned when she pressed her sex against his erection and slowly rubbed against it. The separation caused by their clothes was delicious torture and merely heightened the anticipation.

He moved his mouth to her neck, then her throat, then, finally, to the curve of her breast. She tangled her fingers in his dark hair, wanting more, and cried out when he moved his mouth over her nipple. She jerked against him again, her jeans feeling even more tight against her sensitive flesh. And when he began to suckle her, taking one nipple in his mouth while he teased the other with his fingers, she thought she'd explode right then.

"I think I had more orgasms last night than I've had in my entire adult life," she admitted, giving herself over to the sensations.

Sucking deeper, he surged up against her, mimicking the way they'd make love when their clothes came off. That was all it took to push her over the edge into a shattering climax that made her cry out with the pure, electric pleasure of it.

He kissed her, catching her cry with his lips and tongue, then whispered, "Are we starting over, or does this still count as part of last night? It was after midnight, after all. This might be a day for the record books."

She laughed, her laugh turning to a hungry groan when he pulled his own shirt off, baring his strong, hard body. The soft sunshine spilling into the attic from the grated air vents cast lines of shadow and light across his golden torso, spotlighting the perfect ripples of sinewy muscle.

She leaned down, nibbling that skin, running her tongue along his shoulder to his neck. Then lower, so she could taste one flat male nipple. His hands caressed her bare body to her waist, still toying with her breasts, then playfully dipping below the waistband of her jeans to teasingly caress her. Close. Very close to where she wanted him, but not going all the way, always coming back up, leaving her a quivering mass of need.

"Touch me or I'm going to scream and convince everyone in this place that there really are ghosts here."

"Ghosts usually scream with pain," he replied, still so patient, so deliberate, his hands creating magic wherever he decided to move them. "You'll be screaming with pleasure before the afternoon is out."

She suspected he was right.

11

MILES KNEW he was driving Gwen into an erotic frenzy. Her arousal was almost a tangible thing, he could see it, hear it, smell it, taste it. She swayed in a seductive, mindless dance as she knelt above him, her body responding to his slightest touch, to every move he made. She was ready—beyond ready—wanting nothing more than to proceed directly to the main course and skip the appetizer.

Too bad for her. Miles liked appetizers.

In no hurry, he pulled her closer, until her legs were nearly wrapped around his hips on the chaise. Then he began to kiss her, deeply, intent only on the pleasure of lips and tongue, the way she tasted and smelled. She caught the rhythm of his strokes, meeting him touch for touch.

Moving his hands down her back, he focused on the satiny feel of her skin, the tiny protuberance of bones in her spine, the indentation where waist met hip. Then lower, his fingers slipping inside the back of her jeans to toy with the elastic edge of her bikini panties.

She arched back, curving toward his touch, moaning low and long. He didn't give her what she silently begged for, moving his hands up and away, almost smiling at her nearly inaudible whimper. When she was once more caught up in their deep, slow kisses, he again allowed himself to touch her. This time he brought both hands to the waistband of her jeans, then beneath. He caressed her hips, then lower, until he could cup her sweetly curved rear. He pushed up against her, torturing himself as well because of the constricting tightness of his jeans against his erection.

He might as well have waved a red flag in front of a bull. She needed no more encouragement to go further. Standing, she pushed her jeans off her hips, revealing her soft belly, her curvy hips, and a tiny pair of blue underpants.

Leaving the panties on, she pushed the jeans down. When they became tangled with her shoes she muttered a soft curse. He laughed softly. As she finally dropped her clothes to the floor, she arched a brow. "You're enjoying this?"

"Hell, *yes.*"

Her eyes narrowed. "Two can play," she warned. Naked but for the panties, she returned to the chaise, kneeling between his parted legs. She dropped her hands to his shoulders, almost on all fours, those perfect breasts of hers swaying just out of reach of his mouth. Then she taunted him, brushing her nipple against his cheek, but not letting him have a taste.

"Two can definitely play, Gwen," he mumbled, settling down for some payback that he sensed he was going to enjoy. A *lot.*

So she began to play, as he had, teasing him with drawn-out caresses. The attic began to feel steamy hot. He ached to get rid of the rest of his own clothes, to feel nothing but her skin and her hair, her mouth and her lips. Finally, after kissing every bit of his chest, from throat to waist, she unfastened his jeans and began to tug them off. He lifted up to help her, then kicked off his shoes.

When he was completely naked, she resumed her place on his lap, wrapping her legs around his hips. "Still enjoying this?"

Drawing in a hoarse breath at the feel of her, so close, so

hot, he nodded weakly. "But I think you forgot something." He glanced down at their bodies, nodding toward the skimpy pair of blue panties still separating them.

She shook her head. "I didn't forget." With a look of pure feminine mischief in her eyes, she tilted her hips and began to rub against his erection. Up. Then down. The silky material of her panties was damp with her own arousal, making the frictionless slide that much more intoxicating.

He groaned. "You're killing me."

"Want me to get off?" Her eyes shone with pure heat and he knew she'd chosen her words deliberately.

"Oh, yeah, I want you to get off, babe. I want to *watch* you get off." He tangled his fingers in her hair, tugging her mouth to his for a wet, hungry kiss. When they parted to suck in a few deep breaths, he whispered, "I want you to get off so many times you can't remember your own name."

"I hear that's going around," she whispered with a saucy grin.

"Christ, if that's what caused it, we'd have half the people in the world begging to get amnesia."

Then her laughter faded as her body tensed. Her fingers clenched, then flexed. Her head was tilted back, her eyes closed. She breathed in shallow little gasps, her helpless whimpers telling him how close she was to release.

Holding tightly to her hips, he rocked up against her, rubbing her where he knew it felt the best. He'd never imagined the power, the pure sensual delight of giving this beautiful, responsive woman something hot and hard to pleasure herself with. He loved watching her take what she wanted, bringing herself to the edge. Finally, she shuddered, tightened and gave a helpless little cry.

When she collapsed on to him, boneless and sated, she whispered, "Who am I again? I can't seem to recall."

"Mine," he growled. "That's all you need to remember."

Watching her pleasure herself to climax had pushed Miles as far as he could go. Her flimsy panties separated easily under his hands, ripping apart with one sharp tug. She gasped, then smiled, obviously pleased she'd driven him so far.

"You might want to let me catch my breath," she whispered, still looking weak from her explosive climax. "Looks like I'm in the driver's seat."

"You don't have to do a thing," he promised with utmost confidence. "The pleasure's all mine."

After sheathing himself with a condom he'd tucked into his jeans pocket earlier that day, he lifted her, rocking her against him. Her weight was fully supported in his arms. That wet, warm, feminine flesh of hers slid against his erection in blatant welcome. Dipping inside her, he forced himself to use what little restraint he had left. He wanted to savor the connection, knowing from last night that the physical sensation of having Gwen wrapped around him was like nothing else on earth.

She was having none of that. Out of breath or not, she took over, plunging down to take him, all of him, in one powerful thrust. "Oh, Miles," she moaned. "The pleasure's definitely not all yours."

"You are always in such a hurry," he managed to mutter before he went completely out of his mind. Then he could do nothing but follow his body's instinctive demands. He thrust up into her, again and again, holding her, lifting her, rocking their bodies together in a perfectly timed sexual dance.

They exchanged long, wet kisses. Intimate caresses. And

looking up at her, seeing the ecstasy on her face, watching her give herself over to climax again, he knew he could make love to just this one woman for the rest of his life and die a happy man.

Finally, he couldn't think anymore, couldn't analyze it, could only focus on the pleasure. Gwen obviously got her breath back, because she took over, dropping her feet to the floor on either side of the lounge. She picked up the tempo, set a new pace. Hard and fast. Mind-blowing. Until he could take it no more and exploded into her in one long, shattering release.

GWEN SPENT the rest of the day catching up on the chores she should have been doing that morning. Not that she regretted the way she'd spent her time. No matter what happened at the end of this crazy weekend, she didn't regret a thing.

She and Miles had finally managed to escape the attic at around two. After making love, they'd lain wrapped in each other's arms. Talking about silly things. Sharing laughter, slow kisses and languorous caresses.

Eventually, they'd fallen into a light sleep on the chaise lounge. When they'd awakened, they'd dressed, then checked the elderly couple's room and found it empty. Gwen had been greatly tempted to search their luggage for any counterfeiting equipment, but Miles had convinced her they'd be too smart to bring it along on their vacation.

They'd parted outside his room with a long kiss. Again he'd promised to stay put until she could find Mick Winchester. Again, she suspected he wouldn't do it.

Since Miles had admitted to having a slight headache after their nap, Gwen did want to seek out the doctor. She wasn't able to locate the woman until late that afternoon.

Dr. Wilson came into the house, her arm loosely draped around Mick Winchester's waist. Both of them were laughing.

Gwen couldn't prevent a frown. "Have a nice afternoon out?"

"Wonderful," the doctor replied. "Mr. Winchester showed me some of the sights in Derryville."

Since Derryville was small enough to walk across in an hour...on crutches...that shouldn't have eaten up an entire afternoon. Ordinarily, she might have smiled at the obvious sexual atmosphere between Mick and the lady doctor. Right now, though, she was too concerned about Miles to muster up much amusement.

"How's our patient?" Dr. Wilson asked.

"He's got a slight headache. He's up in his room."

"Still no memory?"

She shook her head with a sigh. "No, I'm afraid not."

Dr. Wilson shrugged, not looking too concerned. "I'm still certain he'll be fine. Did he sleep at all last night?"

Gwen wished her pale skin didn't blush so easily, particularly because Mick appeared to notice. A wide grin told her he'd read her expression correctly.

"Not very well."

"Well, maybe I'll pop in to see him before I take a shower." She patted Mick's chest. "You coming?"

"In a minute," he replied, not taking his eyes off Gwen.

The brunette walked away, heading up the stairs with a definite sway to her hips, obviously intended for Mick's eyes. He stared after her. When she reached the landing on the second floor and turned to look down at them, he gave her a flirtatious wink.

"Do you ever quit?" Gwen muttered.

"The day I do, you better check my pulse," he replied.

She couldn't prevent a slight laugh. "You're such a horndog. I can't believe you're related to Sophie."

He smiled at the reference to his sister, who'd become one of Gwen's best friends here in Derryville. Sophie was the sweetest-natured woman Gwen had ever known, which probably served her well in her job as the secretary of the First Methodist Church. Nothing at all like her brother.

In some ways, though, she was a bit like Gwen. Because, while most people only saw the quiet church secretary, there was more to Sophie than met the eye. The two of them had bonded when Gwen had seen Sophie's bookshelf and realized they shared a taste in reading material. Sophie had an entire collection of books by a rising star in the horror fiction world, R.F. Colt. Gwen had read all of Colt's books back in Boston and was a big fan.

"Growing up with a sister made me that much more aware of how insane a man can get trying to understand women," Mick said. "It's better to just enjoy the ride and not try to make too much sense of it."

"Maybe having *you* for an example explains why she's still single," she said tartly. Since Sophie was very pretty, Gwen had wondered why she'd never settled down with someone special.

"Touché. But my cousin Jared was practically a big brother to her, too. He's a little more responsible about his relationships with women than I am...." He chuckled for some reason. "At least *usually*."

"Sophie's told me about him. Isn't he the true-crime writer?" She knew he was. His books constantly topped the best-seller lists, though Gwen had never read one. She probably would someday, because it sounded like his books were right up her alley. Lately, though, reading had been one pleasure she hadn't had time to indulge.

Mick nodded. "Yeah. He doesn't live around here anymore. But he sometimes pops in when he's least expected."

"I haven't met him yet on any of his visits."

Mick's eyes sparkled with humor. "Nope. But I'm sure you will one of these days. When he...comes around again. I'm afraid he hasn't been himself lately."

Gwen didn't think it likely he'd drop around. Frankly, she didn't *want* to meet the man. From what Sophie had told her, her cousin Jared had a real knack for getting to the bottom of old, never-solved mysteries, figuring out intricate crimes and dragging them back into the light of day for renewed dissection. He was apparently relentless when something caught his interest.

Someone like that sounded like someone she, herself, would have liked to meet in the old days. He was also, however, the *last* kind of person she'd want near Aunt Hildy. No way did she want her aunt talking to a determined author who liked to revisit old scandals and mysteries and write about them. And who, according to Sophie, had a lifelong interest in the history of organized crime in Chicago.

Aunt Hildy didn't deserve to be dragged into the spotlight, raked over the coals, yet again. The woman finally seemed to have found some peace and happiness in her life, and Gwen wouldn't allow anyone to upset Hildy's delicate mental state.

So, no, indeed, she didn't intend for the two of them to ever meet. Mr. Jared Winchester was more than welcome to keep living his rich, high-rise life in Chicago, thank you very much. Gwen hoped he *never* came back to Derryville.

Not that she expected it to happen. From what Sophie

said, her cousin was a dashing, world-traveler who'd made a name for himself in the FBI before he'd ever started writing. He spoke several languages, lived on intrigue, and never spent more than a few months a year at home. Didn't exactly sound like someone who'd be up for hanging out in his old hometown of Derryville.

Gwen changed the subject. "Speaking of coming around, I hope our Mr. Stone does soon. I don't know how much longer I can keep him hidden up there without anybody finding out he's here. And you've certainly been no help."

Mick brought a hand to his chest, looking offended. "I've been working hard to try to prevent the arms dealer from meeting up with his potential buyer."

Her heart skipped a beat. "You know who Miss Jones is?"

"Not definitely," Mick admitted. Then he lowered his voice to whisper, "But I have my suspicions. Why do you think I've been sticking so close to Dr. Wilson?"

"You don't think...but she doesn't have a birthmark!"

"She does have a small scar on her collarbone," Mick replied. "Maybe the birthmark was removed. Speaking of which, I think five minutes is long enough to let her out of my sight."

Gwen felt her blood grow cold. "You sent her up to his room. She's alone with Miles right now. Are you crazy?"

Mick shrugged, looking unconcerned as he turned toward the stairs. "Don't worry about it. I made up a story about how I know who he is and have known him forever. I told her I'd always heard it was better to let people regain their memory naturally. She agreed. She has no idea what he's doing here."

"Someday, you're going to have to tell me how you got caught up in this whole thing," Gwen said, her curiosity temporarily overriding her concern. "If I hadn't been existing on pure adrenaline for the past twenty-four hours, I'd be asking a whole lot more questions."

He paused, his hand on the railing. "Adrenaline, huh? That's the reason why you haven't been asking anything?" He looked skeptical, and curious.

She knew what he meant. Why hadn't she questioned this whole crazy scenario more than she had? A number of times she'd been tempted to reach for the phone, check things out, ask information for the listing to the top-secret agency called the Shop. She could have searched the Internet. Cornered Mick. Called the police. Absolutely anything.

Something had stopped her each and every time.

"What *really* stopped you from figuring out what was going on here this weekend?" he asked, as if he could read her mind.

"I'm not sure myself," she admitted. When he laughed softly, she raised a brow. "What's so funny?"

"Nothing. I'm just amused that you're enjoying the hell out of this. Who'd have ever figured the nice, quiet innkeeper has such an adventurous soul?"

An adventurous soul. She *had* once upon a time. She'd nearly forgotten the dreams she'd had growing up, the thrills she'd always envisioned being a part of her future. The fits she'd given her parents as a teen who'd let her love of excitement overcome her common sense on more than one occasion.

"Is that why *you* got involved?" she asked.

"I'm always up for new and exciting ways to get in trouble."

She crossed her arms and gave him a pointed glance. "And somehow an attractive woman always ends up involved."

"True," he admitted. "Getting to know Dr. Wilson hasn't exactly been a hardship."

"I'll bet."

They began walking up the stairs together. "Speaking of her, you'd better be right. Miles had better be safe with her. He's not in a position to defend himself."

"You don't have to worry about Agent Stone, sweetheart," Mick replied. "He's a tough hombre. Black belt. Weapons expert. Long history of successes."

Not sure she wanted to know the answer, she asked, "Successes?"

Mick paused and met her stare, lowering his voice. "Don't ask. You don't wanna know what that man's done. All, of course, for his country."

She tried to reconcile that dangerous, deadly image with the one of the man dangling against the side of her house earlier today, bemoaning not having any Inspector Gadget-type equipment. The pictures didn't quite match up in her mind. "He's an unusual man." She was speaking more to herself than to Mick.

"Uh-huh. I get the feeling you *like* unusual. Something's different about you this weekend. Excitement suits you."

"Who wouldn't be excited? Secret agents with amnesia? Arms dealers? Mysterious buyers?"

When they reached the second floor, Gwen turned to walk to Miles's room. The door was open, which she figured was a good thing. If Dr. Wilson or Miss Jones or whoever she was had mischief on her mind, she'd likely have closed the door.

Before she could walk away, Mick put a hand on her arm. "I like this new you, Gwen. I hope this sparkle I see in your eyes doesn't go away too quickly."

In spite of his flirtatious charm and sexy playfulness,

Mick was generally a nice guy. She saw a mutual feeling of affection in his expression. "Can I admit I do, too? I guess I'm not quite ready to go back to boring and conservative. I'm liking adventure. A lot." *Probably too much.*

Mick squeezed her hand. "Good. Listen, I'm going to wait for Dr. Wilson in my room. It's probably good that she doesn't see me with, uh, Agent Stone, just in case he suddenly remembers something and blurts it out. Will you tell her where I am?"

She nodded, then waited for him to walk away toward his own room. Standing outside Pretty Boy's Pad, she watched through the open door as Dr. Wilson chatted with Miles, examining his eyes, his balance and asking him memory-related questions.

She took advantage of the moment to stare at him, at this man who'd turned her world upside down in a single day. It amazed her, truly astounded her, that yesterday morning she hadn't known he existed. Because, as crazy as it seemed given their short relationship, she hated the thought of being without him.

It was more than excitement, more than attraction. Though attraction had a lot to do with it. After all, she'd never in her life made love with someone who'd made her forget the rest of the world existed. When she was with Miles, that's exactly what happened. The inn didn't exist. Her guests didn't exist. There was no former fiancé, no ghosts, no Hildy. Just him. His hands. His lips. His tongue. His knowing eyes and sultry whisper.

Miles was the dark, dangerous man of her most secret dreams.

Yet she also *liked* him. She'd liked him before he was hurt, and since they'd spent nearly every hour since then in each other's company, she'd gotten to know him pretty well—even though he didn't completely know himself. But amnesia didn't change the way someone smiled or the things that made him laugh. A knock on the head couldn't disguise the tenderness he'd show to others, the wicked sense of humor, the intelligence and the wit. Nor could it hide the intrinsic goodness in a man. Those things were as much a part of Miles as his full name or birth date, and she'd seen evidence of *all* of them since they'd met.

She liked talking to him, laughing with him, just sitting in a quiet room with him, having a normal conversation, as they had when she'd first shown him up to his room the night before.

That didn't mean she didn't want to know even more. She wanted to know his dreams and his plans, wanted to know what kind of kid he'd been, if he'd terrorized his siblings, what his parents were like. She wanted him to get his memory back because she wanted to learn more about his past. Probably, most of all, she wanted to know if he was going to be a part of her future.

"Get real, Gwen, it's impossible," she whispered, leaning against the wall and tilting her head back in frustration. "This has been an illusion. It would never work."

A fantasy. A dream. That described this whole Halloween adventure pretty well—it had certainly had its share of surreal moments. She dreaded the one when she'd have to wake up and face reality. Because dark, dangerous, worldly men like Miles didn't stick around. Not with small-town innkeepers whose biggest weekly adventure usually involved trying to find good pablano peppers at the tiny local grocery store.

A whirlwind relationship with a dark, dangerous man might suit Gwen fine for a weekend, but it certainly wasn't something they could ever maintain. In the real world, in the mundane existence of Gwen Compton, innkeeper, how would she and Miles find any common ground? How soon would it be before he realized she wasn't the daring woman he thought her to be, and leave for more exciting pastures? When the talk turned from spies to reliable maid service, from weapons to breakfast dishes, how long would it take him to realize he'd made a horrible mistake?

She already mourned the loss of the most passionate relationship she'd ever known. But it was inevitable. Whether Miles stuck around for a few days, or even a week, sooner or later he'd have to get back to his real life. A life she wasn't in a position to share.

Maybe you could *share it,* a voice whispered in her brain.

Impossible. Even if there wasn't the inn to think about, she had to take care of Aunt Hildy. She wasn't free to go off on adventures with a mysterious, jet-setting man. And while she had loved every minute they'd shared, deep down inside, she really didn't want to. Adventures in small doses were one thing, but a lifetime of them? Always on the move to new towns with new risks? Exciting, perhaps, but not very conducive to long-term happiness.

She was twenty-eight years old. While the thrill of physical danger appealed to her now, so did the thought of building a life with someone. Having children. Settling down and creating a home. Taking walks in the fall and camping trips in the spring. Curling up in front of a fire on a cold winter's night and being wrapped in a pair of strong arms when she'd had a bad day.

Finding adventures in everyday things would suit her fine, in the long run. She wanted a normal life in the normal world. Which meant a world that didn't involve trips to foreign lands, gun-carrying secret agents, arms dealers or mysterious buyers.

A world with no Miles Stone.

12

MILES SENSED Gwen had something on her mind that evening. Funny, though he'd only known her a short time, he already felt in tune to her moods and knew when something was wrong.

Throughout the afternoon she'd been every bit as warm, sexy and playful as she'd been since he'd first woken up in the kitchen and had seen her kneeling over him. She'd kept him amused while he was trapped in his room—both for his own good, and because she'd taken all his clothes away to wash them. They'd talked, they'd laughed, they'd teased, they'd even played a game of strip poker. She'd won. After all, he'd had no clothes until an hour ago when she'd brought them back from the laundry room.

But through it all, there'd been a slight reserve, a hint of sadness that hadn't been in her eyes this morning.

He didn't like that look. Miles wanted to sweep it away, to see her glowing with happiness, bouncing with energy, as she had been earlier in the day. And he'd do anything to ease her shoulders of that slight, weary slump.

He had to concede, she wasn't the only one with something on her mind. He was having the same problem. Unfortunately, what was on his mind was *nothing.* Having nothing on his mind—no memories, no clues about his real life, no idea where he lived—could really be a pain in the ass.

Only one good thing had come out of this whole mess.

And she was curled up in his arms on his bed right now, watching the room grow shadowy as the last of the daylight faded away with the sunset.

"You okay?" she whispered against his chest, as if knowing he was deep in thought.

"Fine. Just thinking."

"About?"

Figuring she'd tell him what was bothering her on her own time, he hedged. "About what happens if I don't get my memory back. I wasn't too worried today. Hell, anybody slammed by your Aunt Hildy would have his brain scrambled for a day."

She laughed softly, as he'd intended.

"But I am getting a little concerned about tomorrow. I told Dr. Wilson I'd go to the hospital if I'm not okay by then."

"I think that's a good idea," Gwen replied. Then she added, "Dr. Wilson...you talked with her for quite a while today."

He pulled back to look her in the eye. "You can't possibly be jealous."

"She is very pretty."

"I like blondes."

"How do you know?"

"Okay," he admitted, "I like *you*."

Like, however, didn't quite nail it. What he felt for Gwen already went beyond "like." He didn't know if he was the emotionally impulsive sort. That didn't sound like the kind of person a secret agent would be. But there was no doubt: he *was* developing feelings for Gwen.

He wasn't fool enough to call it love. At least, he didn't *think* he could call it that, particularly because he didn't know whether he believed in love at first sight or not.

Or maybe he did. Maybe that personality trait was locked away in the uncharted territory of his mind and what he was feeling made perfect sense in his normal life.

Reason and logic, however, said love took time. It meant knowing someone, inside and out. Their past, their present and future. Knowing what they wanted out of life, and where they'd come from. Knowing what was important to the other person. Above all, wanting nothing more than to make that other person happy.

Looking at it from that perspective should have convinced him there was no way he could possibly be in love with Gwen Compton. Because he couldn't claim to know any of those things.

With the exception of one. Since he'd opened his eyes and seen her the night before, he'd thought more than once that he'd consider his life successful if he only ever managed to do one thing. Make her happy.

And so far, the happiest he'd seen Gwen, other than the times they'd been making love, had been when they'd been involved in one adventure or another. "You know, babe, as much as I appreciate you taking care of me, I'm going a little stir-crazy locked up in this room."

She lifted a brow.

"I think we should get outta here for a while."

She nibbled her lip, looking greatly tempted. "I have to play hostess during cocktail hour."

"You *have* to?"

She hesitated, then mused aloud. "Well, the hors d'ouevres *are* all prepared. And Aunt Hildy usually makes the drinks."

He had her now. He could practically see the wheels turning in her mind—hmm, boring cocktail hour...or a little outdoor adventure? "Come on," he cajoled. "Let's blow this place."

Gwen finally grinned and nodded. He immediately grabbed her hand and pulled her off the bed.

"Now?"

"Right now. By the time we get outside, it'll be dark."

He was right. After they made their way down a back staircase, which led from the second floor into an area Gwen called the mudroom, they slipped out the back door into a pitch-dark evening. Night had fallen rapidly once the sun had gone down, and without those warm rays, it had grown chilly. He could see his own breath making misty circles in the cold air. He reached over to zip up his leather jacket—which Gwen wore.

"I should have gotten mine," she protested. "You'll freeze."

"I'm fine. We secret agents have thick blood, you know."

She chuckled. "Sure you do. And hard heads."

"Ah-ah, no penny cracks tonight."

"Okay. Um, any idea where we're going?"

He thought about it for a second, trying to let his intellect give way to instinct. Instinct said... "Let's drive."

She nodded, then took his hand and pulled him along the side of the house. She clung to the shadows as if she belonged there, peering around the side of the building before rounding the corner. Miles had to hand it to her—for an innkeeper, she was pretty good at this skulking around stuff.

"The streetlight's on in the driveway," she said in a deep whisper. "We'll have to make a run for my car."

He didn't protest, and made a mad dash with Gwen toward the parking area. She beelined for a little white sedan, but his feet somehow skidded to a stop next to a wicked-looking black sports car that practically sang to him. "Let's take this one."

She stared at him from a few feet away, her eyes wide, reflecting the glow of the lamppost. "Miles, that's not my car."

He couldn't tear himself away, feeling almost compelled to get behind the wheel of this sleek monster and let loose all eight of her cylinders. His fingers curled in anticipation and his heart beat faster. Figuring it was useless, he tested the door handle anyway. Then he smiled. *Fate.* "It's unlocked."

"Miles, no. That car has to belong to one of the guests."

"Which one? Maybe it's the suspect's. If so, we should search it. For clues." *And acceleration rate.*

Knowing he was using twisted logic, he gave her the most reasonable, calm look he could manage. Truthfully, the thought of driving like a bat out of hell under the autumn night's sky, with Gwen at his side, was making the blood pound in his veins. His want was so strong he could almost taste it. He wanted nothing more than to ride with her all night long. Going wherever the road took them. Leaving everything else behind.

"We can't do this." She frowned, obviously trying to look stern. She failed miserably.

He pulled the door open, giving her a look that said *I dare you.*

"No."

"Yes."

"We can't."

"We are."

She tilted her head, thinking about it. "Actually, I don't remember anyone registering a Viper."

He nodded, knowing he had her. "That settles it. If it

wasn't registered, it shouldn't be parked here. Owner's lucky you didn't have it towed." He got in, sitting comfortably behind the wheel. Perfect. He didn't even have to adjust the seat.

Gwen hesitated for one second, nibbling the corner of her lip in indecision. Then she dashed over, opened the passenger side door and jumped in beside him. "This is crazy," she said with an out-of-breath laugh. "We can't steal somebody's car."

"We're just searching it," he said, hearing the note of disappointment in his own voice. "Because unless the driver was a rat-brained moron who left his keys in this baby, we're not going to be able to go anywhere."

She raised a brow and gave him a cheeky grin. "You can't hot-wire it?" The sparkle in her eyes almost dared him to do it. But before he had to, she reached for the sun visor, then flipped it down. A set of keys fell on to his lap.

"Looks like the rat-brained moron *wants* his car stolen," Miles said, not even hesitating. He grabbed the keys, inserted one into the ignition, and started the car. He almost purred as throatily as the engine. "Ever been on a joyride?"

"Once or twice as a teenager," she admitted. "I wasn't always the model of propriety you've been with this weekend."

He almost snorted at that one. "If this is you, the model of propriety, I'd be terrified to be with the Gwen who decides to take a walk on the wild side."

She grinned, looking pleased. Then she reached for the glove compartment. "I still don't know about this. Can I just check the registration to be sure?"

He nodded once, knowing this was a dangerous game they were playing. He didn't necessarily want to get caught boosting a car that belonged to a cop or something.

When she turned to look at him, she wore a puzzled frown. "No paperwork. No registration. No nothing."

He thought about it. And quickly reached the only logical conclusion. "Gwen, this must be *my* car."

She raised a skeptical brow.

"I'm serious. I *know* this car. I've been in it. I've driven it. I can feel it. It makes sense. If I was trying to keep my cover, of course, I wouldn't have left any paperwork inside. You said nobody else had registered it." The more he spoke, the more certain he was of his words. She began to look convinced, and he argued his case home. "Besides, how the hell else could I have gotten here? By parachute?"

They stared at each other, then burst into laughter, both knowing that was an absolute impossibility. Not with his problem with heights.

"So you're the rat-brained moron who left his keys in his sun visor?" she asked with a cheeky grin.

"Musta been planning ahead in case I needed to make a quick getaway," he replied, deadpan.

"Uh-huh. That's your story and you're sticking to it?"

The sparkle in her eyes proved irresistible. "God, I'm crazy about you." Unable to resist, Miles leaned over, slipped his fingers into her hair and tugged her close for a hot, wet kiss. She parted her lips, meeting the thrust of his tongue, tasting him, breathing him, almost climbing into his skin and becoming a part of him. Hell, he suspected she already *was* a part of him.

After he let her go, they stared at each other and each sucked in a few deep breaths. His eyes asked a question. Hers answered a definite yes. They both knew how this ride was going to end.

Then, charged with excitement, adrenaline and a pure sexual rush, he threw the car into reverse and took off.

GWEN HAD NEVER been in a car that went so fast, nor one that was so expertly driven. If there had been any doubt before, there was none now. This was definitely his vehicle. Miles almost talked to the thing, communicating with subtle flicks of his wrist on the gearshift, and slight touches on the steering wheel. Just watching the smooth, choreographed moves made her remember the expert way he used those strong hands of his on her body.

The man drove like he made love. With expert precision.

Her breathing grew labored. She was intensely aware of him. Wanting him again, though it had only been hours since they'd last made love. That kiss had called to someplace deep inside her, ordering the wicked Gwen out to play just one more time.

One more night. If he didn't get his memory back, he was going to the hospital tomorrow. Everything could very well change. If tonight was all they had—all they'd *ever* have, as Gwen had already figured—she was going to wring from it every fabulous moment she could.

The memories would have to last her a lifetime.

She wanted Miles to ride fast and ride hard. Both in the car. And in her. "I want you so bad."

He glanced over, his eyes dark and glittering. She knew without asking that he'd been thinking the same thing. Something about having such power, such speed and energy beneath their bodies, was getting them both even more aroused and ready.

Their ride promised to be exciting. Its inevitable conclusion promised to be explosive.

"Do you know where you're going?" she asked, knowing whenever they got to their destination she'd be hard pressed to stop herself from ripping off his clothes.

"Not a clue. Does it matter?"

"Not a bit."

She truly didn't care where they ended up. In this case, it was the journey that mattered. Each mile that passed beneath the tires of the car was another stroke to her senses. Each movement heightened the anticipation. Every curve was a caress, every rev of the engine another delicious bit of foreplay.

The tension was exquisite as heat rushed through her body and blood filled her sex, making her shift on the seat.

They were alone. They were free. They were away from arms dealers and ghosts, from inns and top-secret agencies. And they were completely in tune with one another, sharing the same urgent, sexual need as easily as they shared the same air in the confined space of the car.

She couldn't wait until they arrived, and yet she never wanted the delicious torture of the drive to end.

Truthfully, she never wanted this night to end.

"I wish it weren't so cold so we could put the top down," she said as she leaned back in the comfortable leather seat. Looking out the window, she watched the miles tick away and the sky begin to clear. What seemed like a million stars came out to play. "What a glorious night."

She gave him no directions and he asked for none, seeming to know instinctively where he was going. They drove briefly on the streets of Derryville, then on the interstate, going much faster than the law allowed. She moaned softly, watching the speedometer climb. Her anticipation climbed with it. Finally, after several minutes, she was unable to stand it anymore. She reached across and dropped her hand on to his leg. "I've got to touch you."

He flinched as if burned, obviously every bit as aroused as she, hanging on by a thin thread of control. "We're getting the hell off this highway," he bit out.

He flicked the turn signal and got off at the next exit, making no sound of protest as she deftly unzipped his jeans. A tiny groan was his only response when she slipped her hand into his pants to trace the outline of his erection through his briefs. He was hard and thick against her fingers, and as she stroked him, she couldn't contain a sigh of anticipation.

Once they were off the highway, on a small country road, Gwen could no longer resist. She'd been wanting to taste him since the night before when he'd come into her bed.

She couldn't wait any longer.

Bending down, she ignored his start of surprise. Not giving him a chance to refuse, she pushed his briefs out of the way, pausing for one second to appreciate the masculine beauty of his sex. Then she put her mouth over him and sucked deeply.

"Gwen!"

The car swayed a little, and slowed to a crawl, but she barely noticed. She continued tasting him, swirling her tongue over the tip of his erection, licking away the moisture as she stroked the length of him with her hand.

"Enough," he exclaimed and the car came to a stop. He pulled her up, catching her surprised, open mouth in a deep, wet kiss.

When they broke apart, he muttered, "Come on." He fumbled for the door handle. Before Gwen even had a chance to ask where on earth they were, he pulled her out of the car. She looked around, realizing they were parked in the woods, on a gravel road. She recognized some picnic tables and a playground and knew they'd somehow ended up at some state park. A nearby sign said it was closed for the season. *Perfect.*

She sensed he wanted to get out of the car for the same

reason she did. The intensity that had been building between them from the start of their ride screamed to be let loose under a million stars and a velvety night sky. Not inside the cramped confines of the car.

He took her mouth again, his kiss ravenous. Their tongues tangled and tasted, gave and took. She barely noticed his hands unfastening her pants. But when she did, she helped him, kicking her sneakers off so she could push the slacks all the way off her body. The night air was cold, but the blood pounding through her veins was at the boiling point. So hot, so primed, she didn't notice the outside temperature.

He watched, his eyes glittering in the moonlight. His own pants were undone, his erection thick and ready, still glistening from the moisture of her mouth. She remembered the way he'd tasted, his smell, the intimacy of what she'd done, and knew she wanted to reenact that particular fantasy another time. If she ever could.

Their stares held as he pulled a condom from his pocket and sheathed himself. Then, before she uttered a word, he picked her up, backing her against a huge old tree. Still protected by his leather jacket, she didn't even feel the rough bark. She could only feel *him*. His warmth. His touch. The almost physical power of his hunger for her.

All her senses were on overload, from the sound of the wind whipping through the mostly bare trees, to the smell of his cologne, to the taste of him that lingered on her tongue. And oh, lordy, the sight of him, that desperate want he couldn't hide, nearly made the strength leave her limbs.

"Hurry, please," she said, desperate to feel him inside her.

She had time to wrap her arms around his neck and tilt to

rub against his erection, wordlessly showing him how wet, how *ready,* she was. Groaning, he grabbed her thigh, hooked it over his hip and drove up into her in one deep, powerful thrust.

All Gwen could do was hold on tight and cry out to the sky as he lifted her other leg and drove into her, deeper, again and again. She'd never felt so frantic, so frenzied, so filled.

"I'm never going to let you go, you know that, don't you?" he said with a groan as they both climbed higher and faster toward that ultimate peak.

Oh, God, how she wished that were true. And for right now, with his hoarse breaths in her ear, his strong arms enfolding her and that thick, hot part of him buried inside her body, she almost believed it was.

HE WOKE UP the next morning with a startled groan, having been jarred from his sleep by a strange, disturbing dream. Gwen had been reaching out for him, trying to catch his hand while she clung to the ladder outside the third-floor window. He'd tried to grab her, to keep her close and make sure she was safe. But her fingers had turned to mist and slipped through his grasp.

Maybe the bad dream hadn't been such a surprise. He certainly hadn't gotten much sleep last night. They'd stayed at the closed park, curled in each other's arms inside the car, talking for hours while the night grew old and the stars more brilliant.

She'd told him about her parents and her childhood. Since he'd been unable to reciprocate, he'd responded by making up outrageous tales of his childhood. She'd joined in and together they'd fabricated an entire history for him. From his birth to a poor but proud farmer in eastern Europe, to his daring defection to the U.S. as a teenager, they'd constructed a background fit for a superspy.

He smiled, remembering the sound of her whisper, her laughter, the way her eyes lit up when she was happy.

So unlike the Gwen he'd just been dreaming about.

He reached toward the other side of the bed to ensure she was there, safe and sound, but realized she was gone. "Gwen?" he called, just as he heard the click of the bedroom door.

Though he was naked, he didn't hesitate. He jumped up and rushed to the door, yanking it open to try to catch her before she went downstairs. He wanted to see her with his own eyes, to make sure that disturbing vision of Gwen falling away from him was replaced by the brightness of her good-morning smile.

Someone was standing right outside the door. But it wasn't his blond-haired lover. The man stared at him, noted his lack of clothes and grinned. "That's one way to start the day, running around naked in a public place."

"Shut up, Mick," he snapped. "I have to find Gwen."

Then he stopped. Realized what he'd said. And to whom he'd said it. Frozen in the doorway, he blinked twice as he stared at the familiar face of his cousin. The truth rushed into his brain. Somehow, while he'd slept, while he'd dreamed, everything had returned to the proper place in his mind.

Jared had regained his memory.

13

"YOU BASTARD."

Jared ran a frustrated hand through his hair as he stared at his rotten, grinning cousin. As soon as Mick had realized Jared had recognized him, he'd pushed him back into his room and shut the door behind them. Jared had taken two seconds to pull on his briefs, then had ordered his cousin to start talking.

Mick had talked all right. When he was done, Jared again muttered, "You rotten bastard."

"You keep calling me that," Mick said with a tsk, "and I'll tell my mama you're casting dispersions on her character."

Jared glared. "She'd call you that herself if she found out. I can't believe you knew all along and you said nothing." He shook his head in disbelief. "You let me run around like a nutjob investigating some poor SOB—who's probably a traveling salesman—because I thought he was an international arms dealer."

"No harm done," Mick said, not losing his grin.

"No harm done! I could have been killed."

"You're exaggerating."

"I was hanging off a third-floor window ledge yesterday afternoon."

Mick had the decency to look concerned. "You're afraid of heights, Jared."

"No shit, Sherlock. Had any loving member of my family

been around to remind me of that fact, I wouldn't have tried climbing up that tree outside my window, risking my neck in the process."

Mick snickered and looked out the window. "Lemme guess...you, uh, climbed up the tree to spy on the guy upstairs?"

"Yeah. The one who probably has a trunkful of vacuum cleaners, not weapons."

"You were supposed to wait and meet me in the gardener's shed at noon. I planned to send Gwen out there, too, and lock you in or something." Mick smiled in reminiscence. "Got sidetracked."

"The old gardener's shed is gone," Jared snapped.

"Just as well I got sidetracked then."

He still couldn't believe what Mick had just admitted. His cousin had been here since Halloween night, had seen him in the kitchen after he'd been hurt. He'd known all along who he was. And he'd stood by and let Jared be convinced he was a frigging secret agent. A frigging secret agent with a stupid-ass name.

Unbelievable. Even for Mick.

"Dr. Wilson swore you'd be fine," Mick said. "Besides, I swear, bro, when I first saw you, I thought it was a joke. I was playing along. I thought you were paying me back for something."

"God knows I'd have enough reason," Jared muttered. "When exactly did you figure out it wasn't a joke?"

Mick shrugged and leaned against the windowsill, his hands in his pockets. "Pretty quickly." When Jared frowned, he quickly continued. "I mean, I *suspected* pretty quickly—when I found that Halloween invitation in your car. And when Anne—Dr. Wilson—confirmed you'd had a blow to the head. But I wasn't sure. There was always the possibility you were playing me."

"The invitation...what happened to the murder party?"

"Why did you think the party was this weekend? I sent that invitation a year ago. You missed a great time—*last* Halloween."

Jared muttered a curse. One more reason to find a better way of handling his mail when he traveled. "I just got it when I came home from Russia on Wednesday. I had no idea it was from last year." When Mick visibly relaxed, as though he thought he was off the hook, Jared pointed his index finger at him. "That doesn't excuse what you did. Jesus, Mick, anything could have happened!"

Mick sat on the end of the bed. "Yeah. You could've had fun for a change. Could've let yourself be the Jared I once knew, instead of the brooding, reserved one you've become." Mick glanced at the rumpled covers, then at the white satin bathrobe lying at the foot of it. He crossed his arms and gave Jared a half smile. "Gee, you could've even gone crazy over a blond-haired innkeeper."

"Bite me."

"I'm sure *she* already has."

"Watch your mouth," he growled. "And leave her out of this."

Jared leaned forward, with his elbows on his knees, and rested his forehead in his palm. Gwen. How on earth was he ever going to explain this to her? After everything they'd done, all they'd shared, he was now supposed to tell her he wasn't the mysterious, exciting man she'd come to know?

"You okay?" Mick asked quietly.

"How am I going to explain this to her?" He looked up. "You know she's going to feel like a fool. And you certainly didn't help, setting yourself up as some local CIA informant."

Mick corrected him. "The *Shop*. I can't believe that didn't tip you off, considering how much you used to read Stephen King."

"It did sound familiar," Jared admitted. "Just not for the right reason. Why did you have to bring Gwen into it?"

"She needed an adventure. Needed it almost as much as you did." Mick shrugged. "I don't think you should tell her yet."

"Oh, there's a solution. Let her keep running around thinking she's got a dangerous criminal in her home." He snorted. "I guess that makes about as much sense as anything else you've ever said."

"Admit it. You're already really crazy about her."

Jared couldn't deny it and didn't even try.

"Then seriously, man, don't tell her." Before Jared could reply, Mick held up his hand. "Hear me out. I've known Gwen longer than you. This is the happiest I've ever seen her. She's loving this. Why not let her enjoy it a little longer? Long enough that when she finds out the truth, she, uh..."

"She what?"

Mick glanced away. "She won't walk away, thinking you're just a typical, run-of-the-mill slob like the rest of us."

Jared smirked. "Speak for yourself."

"Look, she likes Special Agent Miles Stone. Give her the fantasy a while longer. Later, when she cares more, it won't matter that you're really just a boring writer."

Just a boring writer. This from the guy who'd once made his living selling double-wides out at the trailer park by the interstate. "Excuse me if I'm not bowing at your feet as you dispense your great wisdom when it comes to women. If

I'm not mistaken, aren't you the guy who had to hide out in my dorm room for a week during college because *three* girls you were dating found out about each other and came after you? *Armed?*"

"College days. I never have to hide from women now."

"They're probably hiding from you," Jared muttered.

"Gwen always has."

That made him pause. He gave his cousin an inquiring look.

"I made a move or two." When Jared's frown deepened, his cousin continued. "Never got anywhere. *Nobody* who's tried ever got a smile half as bright as the one she's been wearing since yesterday." Before Jared could respond, Mick added, "Yours has been absent lately, too, by the way. Until this weekend. So maybe you shouldn't screw this up by coming clean...at least not yet."

No way. There was no way in hell he could continue this charade. Jared hated dishonesty. Truly loathed it. Interacting with criminals both in the FBI and in his writing had given him a hearty distaste for all liars. Damned if he'd allow himself to become one. He'd tell Gwen the truth as soon as he saw her.

"Jared, look," Mick continued, obviously seeing by his expression what he intended to do. "Gwen wants the excitement of Miles Stone. She wants to walk on the wild side, live on the edge. Sure, you're a hell of a guy, but if she finds out you're some reclusive book nut who's fascinated by blood spatter and entry wounds, the interest might fade away pretty fast."

He didn't even want to listen to his cousin, didn't want to consider that he might be right. He and Gwen had shared too much in their short acquaintance for it to be about nothing but thrills. She'd known the real man, even before he'd remembered who that man was. Finding out he had a different job wasn't going to drive the woman away. He was sure of it.

Standing, he ran a hand through his hair. "I need a shower. And I need some other clothes. Get my suitcase out of my trunk, will you? The keys are in the visor." He winced, realizing he had, indeed, taken his own damn car on a joyride the night before.

"No problem." Mick was obviously eager to make up for being such a louse. "I have your wallet in my room. I'll bring it, too." He grinned. "Want me to bring my special shoe phone so you can check in with the Chief and Agent 99 back at headquarters?"

"Screw you and the horse you rode in on, pal," Jared said as he ushered his cousin out the door into the hall.

Mick walked away, but before Jared could shut the door behind him, he noticed Gwen's aunt standing across the hall. She looked curious, obviously having overheard Jared and Mick.

She gave Jared a visual inspection, then winked in appreciation. "You're looking better, Mr. Secret Agent." The old woman's stare grew knowing. Before he could say a word, she continued. "You have your memory back, don't you?"

He nodded.

"Feeling pretty silly right about now, I'd presume."

"What do you mean?"

"Well, Mr. Winchester, if I'd been running around thinking I was a spy, climbing up buildings, breaking into rooms and stumbling into the beds of innocent innkeepers by mistake, I'd probably be rather embarrassed."

He froze, completely stunned. Here was another person in this crazy house who knew who he was and yet let him make a total fool of himself? Even worse, she knew a *lot* about what had been going on. "How long have you known?"

"Didn't recognize you at first. Then yesterday, Moe told me he thought you looked like the fella on the back of one of the books Sam lent me. Pulled it out, there you were."

"Sam?"

"Your grandpa. He and I, well, we keep company."

His *grandfather?* And *Hildy?* "You...keep company?"

She winked and gave a little cackle. "We get together once or twice a week for a can of soup and some slap and tickle."

Yikes. He scrunched his eyes shut and pictured crime scene photos, trying to kill the visual image her words inspired. Then he thought about what else she'd said. "Grandfather gave you one of my books? I didn't think he acknowledged I'd written them."

She blew out an impatient puff of air. "Silly man. He's proud as a peacock of you. Just too stubborn to admit it." She turned to walk away. "I have to go up to the attic for something." Before she left, she gave Jared a speculative look. "Moe tells me you and Gwen had fun up there yesterday. And he said the two of you forgot something." She crinkled her brow. "Something silky and blue. Wonder what that could be." Appearing unconcerned, Hildy gave him a little wave, then walked away.

Jared remembered Gwen's torn underwear less than ten seconds later. Groaning, he yanked on his jeans and shirt and hurried after Hildy, hoping her eyesight wasn't as sharp as her wit.

One good thing—at least this time he'd be going into the attic via stairs and a door, not a tree and a closet.

MILES HAD BEEN MISSING for hours, and Gwen was growing desperate. "Where are you?" she whispered as she stood in his room, having come back here after searching the house yet again.

She'd come up to bring him breakfast at nine and found his room empty. His clothes had disappeared, but his shoes were still on the floor and the bed was a rumpled mess.

This didn't look good.

"Somebody's got him." The suspect must have figured out who Miles was and taken him somewhere. Probably at gunpoint.

She had to *do* something. She would have gone to Mick for help, but she'd seen him leave with Dr. Wilson an hour ago and they hadn't returned. So it was up to her.

Taking a deep breath, she quietly made her way upstairs to the third floor. The elderly counterfeiters had checked out this morning, paying with a credit card that had been approved, thank goodness. Gwen passed the open door to that room and made her way to Capone's Hideaway, the suite where the arms dealer was staying. She listened outside the room for a minute, then knocked lightly. No answer. Praying the man wasn't wide-awake, just ignoring the knock, she opened the door and entered the room.

"Damn." It was empty. She didn't know whether to be relieved she hadn't come face-to-face with the suspect, or disappointed that she couldn't order him to take her to Miles.

Hoping she might find a clue to Agent Stone's whereabouts, she decided to conduct a quick search. She hadn't gotten past the dresser when she heard someone enter.

"What is the meaning of this?" someone asked in a foreign-sounding accent.

Busted! She twirled around, eyes wide, knowing she was no match for this older guy, whether he was armed or not.

He had at least fifty pounds on her, and stood between Gwen and the exit.

Stupid. She should have thought to bring Miles's tiny silver gun, or at least have checked to see if it was still in his jacket pocket. But no, she'd been the blond bimbo in the horror flick going up the stairs toward the danger in the attic. Gwen had never been more disgusted with herself.

She thought fast, quickly arriving at a possible way out. She had one shot at this, one chance at both getting away from this guy and finding out where he'd stashed Miles.

"I'm Miss Jones," she whispered. Well, that sounded pretty pathetic. She took another deep breath, trying to calm her racing heart. "I've been waiting for my chance to meet with you."

Tossing his hat on to the bed, the elderly gentleman tilted his head in confusion. "I thought your name was Miss Compton."

Clearing her throat for courage, Gwen stepped closer. "That's what everyone thinks. But I'm really...um, you know, Miss Jones." Reaching her hand up as if to toy with her necklace, Gwen quickly gave herself a sharp pinch above her collarbone. She bit back a wince, then tugged her sweater to the side to show him the reddened spot, hoping he'd mistake it for a birthmark. "See?"

"Are you quite all right, Miss Jones?" He stared at her as if she had two heads. "Is there someone I could call for you?"

If Gwen didn't know better, she'd swear he had no idea what she was talking about. But she *did* know better. "It's okay, you don't have to pretend. We both know why we're here."

He merely quirked a brow, looking confused, but now also a bit intrigued. "We do?"

"Yes. So let's talk business. I want to buy a...a...gun."

His jaw dropped.

A gun? Twit! Arms dealers sell guns in bulk!

"I mean, a bunch of guns," she quickly clarified. "A whole boatload of them. Highest quality. Um, you know, bazookas, that kind of thing. The best you've got. Money's no object. But you, uh, you know, before we make a deal, you should tell me what you did with the guy who's been tailing us." She shrugged, trying to look as if she didn't really care, one way or the other. "Strictly as a sign of faith."

The man looked stunned, but before he could say a word, they were both startled by a banging coming from the corner. Gwen swung around to see Miles, followed by her Aunt Hildy, emerging from inside the closet.

"Gwen, don't!"

"Miles?" She rushed to him, noting the dust on his clothes and his bare feet. "He locked you in the attic?"

"Would someone care to tell me what's going on here?" the indignant-looking gentleman said. "Should I call the police or the madhouse?"

"Neither!" Miles and Hildy said at the same time.

"Gwen, he's not who you think he is," Miles said.

Aunt Hildy began to laugh. She lifted her quivering fingers to her lips and her eyes twinkled in merriment. "Oh, my goodness, Gwen. You told him you were the mafia buyer? When Moe told me that, I laughed so hard I was afraid I'd finally have a need for those old lady diapers."

Gwen barely spared Hildy a glance. "Miles, where have you been? I've been worried sick."

"Who, exactly, did she think I was?" the older gentleman mused to no one in particular.

"Oh, this is rich," Hildy said with a snorty chuckle. "She

thought you were an international criminal. An arms dealer."

The man's eyes grew wider.

"It gets better. She was impersonating your customer to try to help him." She jerked her thumb toward Miles. Then she snorted another laugh. "The secret agent."

The man sat down on the edge of his bed, looking dazed.

Gwen began to feel a fluttering of unease in her stomach. The way Hildy was talking, some major confusion had been going on around here. And she still hadn't figured out why her aunt and Miles had been in the attic. "What's going on, Miles?"

He shook his head, as if he didn't know what to say, or where to begin. Finally, he spoke, addressing the man on the bed. "I am so sorry you were dragged into this, sir. I had an accident Friday night, got hit on the head and ended up with short-term amnesia. For a variety of reasons, which I won't go into now, I became convinced I was a..." He looked away, his face growing flushed. "A, uh...secret agent in search of an arms dealer."

The man gave a tiny smile, pointing to his own chest. "Me?"

Miles nodded.

"I, Ricardo Tavares, an arms dealer? How utterly delightful." He chuckled. "Was I a dangerous sort of fellow?"

"Deadly."

"Even better. And the lady?"

"She thought she was helping. She was posing as a buyer."

"Ahh." The man's lips twitched. "A bazooka, indeed."

"He's not him?" Gwen asked, feeling like a complete idiot for confronting one of her own guests in his room.

At least Mr. Tavares appeared to be taking the whole thing well.

Then she started really paying attention to what Miles had said. He'd *thought* he was a secret agent?

"I woke up this morning and remembered the truth." Miles turned to face Gwen, giving her a look so full of regret and tenderness, she almost didn't hear what he said next. God, she hadn't even begun to realize how much this man meant to her until she'd feared something terrible had happened to him.

She never wanted to feel that way again. *Never.*

"Why didn't you come tell me you had your memory back?" She wanted both to punch him and hug him tight enough to break. "Instead you just disappeared. You scared me half to death!"

He shook his head with regret. "I'm so sorry. Hildy and I got caught up with what we were doing." Before she could ask him exactly what that had been, he continued. His words made her forget everything else. "I'm not Miles Stone, honey. I'm not a secret agent. There's no mission, no suspect, no Miss Jones."

Her heart skipped a beat as she struggled to suck air into her mouth. "*None* of it was true?" she asked in a thin whisper.

"No," he admitted. "I got an invitation to a Halloween murder weekend held in this place *last* year. Somehow the mail got messed up. I've been out of the country, and it was waiting for me when I got home. I thought it was for this weekend, so I came in character."

Still stunned, she mumbled, "Mick's party. He told us about it right after we moved to town."

"Right. I was supposed to be coming as a secret agent. I thought, when we met in the kitchen, I assumed you..."

Everything began to make sense. "You thought I was a guest at the party, too."

"Exactly."

Good lord. He'd been playacting, thinking she was doing the same. He'd assumed she was a guest, also pretending to be someone she wasn't. They'd been two strangers sharing a fanciful interlude in a haunted house on Halloween, both completely mistaken about who the other had been. If it weren't so unbelievable, it would almost be charming.

Then, of course, the night had gone from unbelievable to surreal. "Aunt Hildy's pennies..."

"I really did have amnesia." He swept his hand through his hair in visible frustration. "Mick recognized me right away and thought it would be just hilarious to let me run around like a lunatic for a couple of days. I could kill him."

"You're gonna have to stand in line," Gwen snapped.

She turned away, looking at her own hands, which were tightly clenched in front of her.

Special Agent Miles Stone didn't exist. The dangerous, dashing adventurer, who had swept her off her feet and given her the most passionate weekend of her life, had been nothing but a figment of her imagination. And his own.

She waited for the rush of relief, waited to be glad he wasn't a daring thrill-seeker who would be whirling out of her life as quickly as he'd whirled into it. Part of her *was* glad. Thrilled, really, that he might, just *might* be the kind of man who'd stick around.

Another part of her was utterly terrified.

Gwen had let herself get caught up in this, had gone full speed ahead into a reckless adventure, always keeping the knowledge in the back of her mind that it would never last. It would be one daring fling she could remember all her life, long after Agent Miles Stone had swept out of it. And after he'd gone, she could go back to her safe, self-protected world. Not allow herself to be vulnerable. Keep her heart closely guarded.

But there was no Agent Miles Stone against whom she could harden her heart for her own self-preservation. There was only this man, whose name she didn't even know. And if he stayed, she might just be forced to take the biggest risk of all.

The risk of letting herself love him without fear, without reservation.

She waited for a second, absorbing that thought, then found herself imagining it. Picturing it all happening. Them being together. Him being a normal, stick-around kind of guy who'd be happy with a quiet life here in Derryville. With her.

Oh, please, God, let him be a schoolteacher. Or an insurance salesman. Or a minister.

Before she could fantasize any longer, he continued. "I saw Mick this morning and recognized him right away. That's when I realized my brain had started working again sometime during the night. I was going to find you, to tell you the truth." He glanced at Hildy and gave her a rueful smile. "Then I ended up going into the attic with your aunt. We got, uh, sidetracked."

"Sidetracked?"

"Showed him some of my old pictures," Hildy explained matter-of-factly. "This boy knows his history."

A feeling of dread—the same one Gwen always experienced when someone got too close to Hildy and started asking too many questions—rose inside her. "Does he?"

"Your aunt has had a fascinating life. Utterly fascinating."

She stiffened, unable to help it. A lifetime's worth of protectiveness toward her elderly relative made her give her lover—her dark, dangerous, exciting lover—a cool stare. But before she could even begin to assess how much of a problem this could be, there was one more thing she had to know.

"Okay," she said, "so you're not a secret agent. This entire weekend has been a...a Halloween game." That wasn't so far from the truth. They had, indeed, been role-playing their way through a mystery party weekend. They just hadn't realized it. "But I really would like to know one thing."

"Yes?"

She crossed her arms, mostly to try to remain aloof, at least until she found out what she needed to know. She was almost afraid to ask, because a little niggling suspicion had begun whispering in the back of her mind. She thrust it away.

"Who are you?"

He didn't reply for a second. She noted the way his shoulders stiffened the tiniest bit. He took a deep breath, as if unsure what her reaction would be to learning his true identity. Considering how tangled her emotions were, and figuring his were the same, she couldn't entirely blame him.

"I'm Mick's cousin. Jared Winchester."

She allowed his words to echo in her mind for a second. Her lover's name wasn't Miles, it was Jared. Jared was the man who'd made such exquisite love to her. Jared was the name she *should* have been whispering while their bodies were joined in the most intimate way possible. Jared had made her laugh and held her close, had teased her and seduced her. Jared had hauled her through that window, had taken her madly last night under the stars, had given her the adventure of a lifetime.

Jared. Jared Winchester.

Oh, God.

Not a simple schoolteacher. Or a salesman. This was *worse* than when she'd thought him a secret agent. Because, from what she knew of him, Jared Winchester was every bit the world-traveling, danger-loving, dark and daring man Miles Stone had been. Not the kind of man to be content living in a small country inn, settling down, getting married, raising kids.

And there was, of course, one additional, *huge* drawback.

"You write those books," she whispered.

His shoulders stiffened. His dark brown eyes suddenly looked cool as he gave her one brief nod. He said nothing else, waiting for her to react. She saw the way his fingers were clenched against his sides, saw the beating of his pulse in his temple and knew, simply *knew,* the ball was in her court. Their future was up to her. Whatever happened next was in her hands, whether they continued to be together or not.

Yes, she'd only known him a matter of days, but she knew, deep in her heart, that she'd already fallen in love with him. Maybe the Gwen she'd been last week wouldn't have allowed it. Certainly she wouldn't have admitted it. But the Gwen she'd rediscovered since the moment she'd met him knew it was true.

She loved his wit and his sense of adventure. She loved his tenderness toward her, his smile, his laugh. She loved the way he looked at her, the way his arms felt wrapped around her. She loved doing nothing more than talking to him for hours. He was intelligent, charming, funny and crazy about her. Everything she'd ever thought she wanted in a man.

A part of her screamed to let him stay, to get to know the real man, as well as the shadowy reflection she'd fallen for.

But she couldn't.

She had no more of a future with Jared Winchester, the world-renowned writer, than she'd had with Miles Stone, the dashing adventurer. She couldn't even let herself steal just a day or two more with him.

Because of Hildy. Because of what he'd already learned and what he might discover. Because of what he might eventually want to do with that knowledge and how it would affect her great-aunt.

But the main reason she had to end it now was that if she didn't make him go, now, she might find herself in the pathetic position of begging him to stay, later.

"Gwen?" he asked, his voice tender, his expression so patient and open it hurt her to look at him.

Blinking rapidly to keep tears from falling from her eyes, she glanced away.

"I think it's time for you to leave."

14

JARED KNOCKED on his grandfather's door one hour later. It had hurt like hell to just pack up and walk away from the inn. But he'd had to do it.

Maybe Mick had been right. Maybe Gwen had wanted the superspy, the adventurer, not the boring writer. That had been the first thought that had crossed his mind when she'd asked him to go.

Now, however, Jared wasn't so sure. Her eyes and voice had held such sadness. She'd refused to look at him after making her request, instead turning her attention to Mr. Tavares. After offering one more apology and an invitation for him to return for a free stay, she'd taken her aunt's arm and led her away. She'd been nowhere to be found when he'd left the house, and he figured she was avoiding him.

"She wanted Miles Stone the adventurer," he'd told himself as he got into his car and sped away from the Little Bohemie Inn, driving even faster and more recklessly than he had the night before. "Not Jared Winchester the murder-obsessed writer."

Eventually he'd slowed down and begun to think. Things didn't add up. He knew her too well to believe she wanted only the fantasy man, not the real one.

She wanted him all right, he had no doubt of that.

But something was holding her back. Something had made her refuse to even give them a chance at making something work in the real world. He'd give anything to know what that something was, but he couldn't press her. He had to give her time to figure things out, to get past the embarrassment and confusion.

They'd been together nonstop for almost two days, it was time to retreat to separate corners and evaluate just what had happened, and how deeply entangled their emotions already were. For himself, he could admit they were pretty damn entangled.

In the meantime, he had *another* relationship to resolve.

He lifted his hand to knock on the door again, but it was opened before he had to. "Hello, Grandfather."

"Hildy told me you'd probably be stopping by," Grandpa said, not stepping aside or asking him in. Though he hadn't seen the elderly man in a couple of years, he didn't notice too much of a change in his appearance. Still tall and gaunt, white-haired and hawk-nosed, Samuel Winchester had been the most formidable police chief this town had ever seen. Though his shoulders were now slightly stooped, and his body more frail than Jared remembered, he maintained a presence that demanded respect.

Their eyes met for a long moment, then finally Samuel Winchester cracked a tiny smile. "Hear you had yourself an adventure this weekend."

Hildy. The woman had probably been on the phone within two minutes of his departure from the inn. "That's quite a girlfriend you have there," he retorted.

"Ayuh," Grandfather replied. Then he stepped aside and beckoned Jared in. "She's a firecracker, that one. Took some serious courting before she'd agree to step out with me."

Jared wondered if his grandfather knew just how much of a firecracker. He still couldn't get over some of the stories Hildy Compton had told him during their long excursion into the attic of the Little Bohemie Inn. She'd dug out pictures, old newspaper articles, telling him firsthand stuff about prohibition and the gangster age that he'd never even dreamed of hearing. It had been fascinating. Thrilling. And some of it very heartbreaking.

He sincerely hoped the woman would someday be honest with Gwen. She deserved to know the truth.

"Want some tea?" his grandfather asked as he turned and led him into the living room of his small house.

Tea. Samuel Winchester's drink of choice for as long as he could remember. They'd shared many cups before Jared had left Derryville. "Yes, I'd like that."

While Grandpa went into the kitchen to make the tea, Jared walked around the living room, noting what had changed and what had not. Though the big-screen television was new, the furniture was exactly the same. His grandmother's sewing basket still sat on the coffee table, as if she'd be mending in front of the TV tonight, though she'd been gone for many years.

He soon found himself standing in front of a loaded bookcase. To his surprise, he saw exactly what Hildy had told him he would—copies of every one of his books. More than one of each, in fact. "I'll be damned," he whispered.

"Your last one was my favorite. I liked the dedication."

Jared didn't turn around, only nodding his acknowledgement. He'd dedicated the book to law enforcement officers everywhere, but two in particular. His father and his grandfather.

"I'm proud of you, Jared. It's not easy for me to say, but I swore if you ever showed up at my door, I'd tell you." He cleared his throat. "I'm sorry. I didn't understand. I thought... I was afraid you'd never come back." His voice trailed off, and Jared had to strain to hear him. "I didn't want to lose you. Your grandmother had died the year before, your sister had just married. Mick was off in college. I felt like my family was slipping away."

Jared slowly turned around and saw Samuel Winchester standing in the doorway. The afternoon sunlight spilling in through the open curtains made his hair glow white and his skin look translucent. He was watching Jared intently, a sheen of moisture unmistakable in his eyes.

When he extended his hand to offer the cup of tea, Jared stepped closer. The cup rattled slightly in the saucer.

His grandfather's hand was trembling.

He'd never seen Grandpa nervous. Not once in his life. Jared took the cup and saucer and placed them on the table, then straightened to look the elderly man in the eye. "Do you think we can start over?"

His grandfather gave one short nod.

"Good," Jared said softly, placing his hand on the old man's shoulder. "Because I plan to stick around for a while. And I think I need your advice on how to court one of those Compton women."

GWEN WATCHED the last of their paying guests pull away, down the long driveway on to the road leading toward downtown. Their first weekend at the Little Bohemie Inn had been a grand and glorious success, as far as most of their visitors had been concerned. And they already had reservations for at least some of the rooms for all the remaining weekends of the year. Including, surprisingly enough, one from Mr. Tavares, who had taken being mistaken for an international arms dealer with exceptionally good humor. Thank heavens for that. She hadn't figured one bad experience would ruin a fledgling inn. After all, how far could the word of mouth of one person go? But she didn't want anyone leaving here feeling upset or unhappy.

Gwen was already feeling unhappy enough for all of them.

Rubbing a weary hand over her brow, she made her way upstairs, deciding to lie down for a little while in the guest room where she'd been staying. Lord, it seemed like a lifetime ago when she'd first gone up there after the flood in her own room. So much had happened. Her whole world seemed to have changed in just two short days.

How was it possible for someone to lose her heart so fast? Realistically, it shouldn't have happened. But logic and realism couldn't explain the thrill she got when she closed her eyes and pictured everything she and Miles—Jared—had shared.

The ache in her heart at probably never seeing him again certainly couldn't be erased by logic. "He only did what you said you wanted him to do, nitwit," she muttered.

He'd left because she'd asked him to go. And she *had* asked him, even though a big part of her had hoped he'd stay. Deep down, she could admit that she'd half wanted him to refuse to leave, to fight for what they had.

She was being as wishy-washy as a kid, and she knew it. The man wasn't a mind reader. She'd drawn the line and had only herself to blame because he hadn't crossed it.

Besides, maybe he hadn't *wanted* to work things out. Maybe once he'd gotten his memory back, he'd remembered he had a girlfriend somewhere. A more exciting life. More interesting people to see, or journeys to take. A world that would never involve a simple innkeeper from Illinois with leaky pipes, ghosts in her basement and a matchmaking elderly relative.

Telling herself that it was for the best, that all fantasy adventures had to end sometime, didn't help. This was bad.

Worse than her broken engagement. Because this time, it wasn't her pride that had taken a hit. It was her heart.

She really *had* fallen in love. Too fast. Without common sense or reason. But there it was.

When she arrived upstairs, instead of going back to her temporary room, she pushed into the one where he'd been staying. Pretty Boy's Pad. Somehow, she just wanted to breathe the air he'd breathed and curl up on the bed where he'd slept.

It wasn't until she was inside, shutting the door behind her, that she realized the room was freezing cold, as if someone had not only left a window open but had also been running the air conditioner full blast.

And one more thing. It wasn't empty.

"Hiya, doll."

Gwen froze, spotting the unfamiliar man sitting in a chair by the firmly closed window. He appeared completely relaxed, sprawled back in the chair, legs crossed with one ankle on the other knee. He was gazing out the window, watching the clouds floating by in the late afternoon sky as if he'd just been killing time waiting for her to arrive.

"Who are you? What are you doing here?"

He didn't get up, but merely shrugged and turned to stare up at her. He gave her a little smile. "I'm a friend a' Hildy's."

If he'd been at all misty or eerie, she would probably have had a quick, crazy thought that he meant one of Hildy's ghost friends. But this guy was solid, even though he looked out of place. "Hildy's downstairs."

"I know." His expression softened. "She's tired. Too much excitement. We'll let her rest, okay?"

She nodded warily, still not entirely sure what she'd

stumbled into here. Some costumed character Hildy had hired to entertain at the inn, perhaps? They had, indeed, discussed hiring costumed performers to serve cocktails or just to mingle with the guests, to add to the aura of the gangster days.

She wondered where Hildy had found him. Because, on this guy, the gangster look definitely worked. He wore a dark blue suit, with wide lapels and white pinstripes. The tie was also wide, shiny, a brilliant scarlet color that most men today would never wear. On his head was an old-fashioned hat, the kind she'd seen in pictures from her grandfather's era. Funny white material covered the tops of his shiny black patent leather shoes—spats, she believed. And he had a couple of large rings on each hand.

"Halloween was two days ago," she murmured. "But this look really does work for you."

"I ain't in costume, sweetheart. Sit down, take a load off. We got some talking to do."

"Is this some kind of audition? Are you an actor?"

He laughed, a deep belly laugh filled with genuine humor. His amusement made his amber brown eyes sparkle. His smile was broad, and she focused on it, noting the sensual fullness of the man's mouth. He had a young Marlon Brando mouth, with sexy lips that practically swore he'd be a good kisser. That might've explained why Hildy had let him into the inn for an audition. He was exactly her great-aunt's type.

"Nah, I ain't no nancy-boy actor. Sit down, kitten, and tell me what you were thinking ordering your man outta your house."

Her mouth dropped open. He was talking about *Jared?* "What business is it of yours?"

He shrugged. "Let's say I got a vested interest. Lemme guess. You think you're protectin' Hildy."

Gwen's eyes narrowed. The man knew too much. "Look, I don't know who you are, but I'm not going to discuss my personal life with you." Intending to go downstairs and ask Aunt Hildy who this man was, and why she'd left him alone in one of the upstairs bedrooms, she reached for the doorknob.

"You're not doing her any favors," he said softly, before she could turn the knob. "All you're doing is finishing the job her family started on her more'n sixty years ago. Taking away the last little bit of herself she's got left. Making her feel bad about it, like she has to hide. Like her parents did." Disappointment laced his voice, and it almost made her ashamed for some reason. "Funny, I woulda thought you loved her enough to want to let her be who she really is for once in her life."

She slowly turned around and stared at him. "Okay, I want to know who you are, mister. Tell me now, or I'm calling the cops."

HE'D GIVEN HER a few hours to think things through, but by four o'clock, Jared had waited long enough. Promising his grandfather he'd return later, he went up to the Little Bohemie Inn. Undeterred by the locked front door, he retraced his steps from Friday night and went around back. The kitchen door was open, and he let himself in, determined to get Gwen to talk to him, to tell him what she was afraid of, so they could both address it and see where they'd go from here.

The house was empty and quiet. His own footsteps on the hardwood floors were the only sound, other than the ticking of the antique grandfather clock in the foyer. He went up the stairs, figuring she was cleaning now that the guests were gone.

Before he began searching, he heard a voice coming from one of the rooms. Gwen was speaking to someone. Funny, he heard her voice in conversation, but he didn't hear anyone else's. He paused, prepared to wait until she was finished. But when she began to sound angry, he tensed. Hearing her threaten to call the cops pushed him over the edge. He burst into the room, almost barreling right into her. "Gwen, are you all right?"

When she saw him, a flash of pure pleasure crossed her face before she could disguise it. That, more than anything, convinced him he'd done the right thing in coming back today. She quickly hid her smile and averted her gaze, but there was no hiding the way her body moved as she pulled in a few deep breaths.

"Hey, sonny boy, 'bout time you got back here."

That was when he noticed the man in the chair by the window. It took about ten seconds for the face to sink in, for his features to register. Jared's heart skipped a beat and his jaw dropped open. "Son of a..."

"Shh." The man in the chair raised a finger to his lips. "Me 'n' Gwen were just having a talk, but since it involves you, ya might's well stick around."

"I have no idea who he is," Gwen said, looking frustrated, but also curious. "But he seems to know a lot about us."

Jared knew who he was. It was absolutely impossible, but he *knew* who he was looking at. He'd seen dozens of pictures of the man only this morning. In the attic of the Little Bohemie Inn.

"Did Hildy hire you to play some kind of matchmaking pranks around here this weekend? Were you supposed to haunt this place or something for Halloween?" Gwen asked.

The man laughed in pure delight and Jared took a moment to focus. He blinked a few times, concentrating on drawing some of the freezing cold air in the room into his lungs in slow, steady breaths. He needed to regain his balance and equilibrium, because he was feeling damned dizzy right about now. This *couldn't* be happening. And yet it was.

"Nah, I'm not the one who's supposed to haunt this place," he replied, grinning. "That's Moe's job. He was the matchmaker, too. He's the one who switched the signs on your rooms."

"Moe?" Gwen sounded skeptical. "Six Fingers Moe?"

The man nodded.

"I think I've heard enough," she said.

"Wait, Gwen," Jared told her, reaching out to take her arm. She didn't pull away, simply meeting his gaze, her amber eyes full of emotion and vulnerability. "Maybe we should listen."

"Damn right you should listen. Do you know how much trouble it was setting you two up? Now you're gonna louse it up because *you*," he pointed to Gwen, "think he's some world-traveling adventurer who won't be happy here." Then he looked at Jared. "And *you* think she only wanted you because she thought you were some johnny-law who lives on the edge." He held out his hands, palms up, gesturing to them both. "That about sum it up?"

When neither of them answered, the stranger rolled his eyes. "I thought so. Here's what youse do...how's about talking for a change? Not swinging from windows like champ'nzees, or hiding out in the attic. Just talk. Believe me, it ain't as sappy as it sounds."

Jared looked at Gwen, wondering if she'd figured out yet what was happening here. She, however, wasn't watching the stranger, she was focused entirely on Jared. "You thought I only wanted Miles Stone, the adventurer?"

Jared met her stare evenly. "Mick gave me that impression, and when you told me to go, I suspected he might be right." Then he raised a brow. "And you really thought I live some wild, dangerous existence as a world-traveling writer?"

She nodded once. "Your cousin Sophie once told me that you hated Derryville, and wanted to see the world. That you'd never be content here."

"I see."

"We all see," the stranger said, sounding bored. "You were both wrong, so get over it and move on."

The man stood, glancing out the window once more. Again Jared questioned his own senses. "You make it sound so easy."

Gwen cleared her throat. "Maybe it is that easy."

Looking down at her, he saw something in her expression that hadn't been there a few moments before. Unreserved emotion. Hope. And maybe even love. "Yeah," he agreed softly, unable to contain a smile. "Maybe it is."

"One more thing before I buzz outta here." The stranger looked at Gwen. "Stop protecting Hildy. Whaddaya think made her so unhappy that she got a little nutty, huh? Those shrinks...*pfft*. If they'da let her tell the truth sixty years ago, maybe she could've moved on, lived a reg'lar life." He stepped closer. "Ask her, toots. Ask her what she wants. And don't hold it against *him*," he pointed to Jared, "if she decides she wants somebody to tell her story." Then he smiled. "You're a good broad. Got a lotta heart. A lot like your grandma."

Jared heard Gwen's startled gasp and realized, at that moment, that she'd begun to understand. She'd pieced things together and arrived at the correct conclusion.

"Tell Sam, your grandpa, I said hello," the man said to Jared. "Best man I knew in this town. He was the first one showed up't my door, telling me he knew who I was, but since I did my time in the joint, he figured my debt was paid. Damn good poker player, too, your grandpa."

"You're...you're..." Gwen's face was pale and Jared reached out and took her hand. Her skin was cold, her fingers shaking. He stepped closer, slipping an arm around her shoulder and pulling her tightly against him.

"So long," the stranger said. Then he walked to the door and opened it. Before leaving, he turned and smiled at them again. "Think I'll go say one last goodbye to Hildy. Tell her this Ghost and Mrs. Muir crap has gotta stop. Ain't healthy for her now that she's got old Sam in her life." Then he pointed to the chair where he'd been sitting. "I left something there. Have a look."

He tipped his hat. "See ya around."

Without another word, Nathaniel Marsden stepped through the doorway.

And disappeared.

GWEN REMAINED FROZEN, taking strength and comfort from Jared's solid arm and warm body. Her head was spinning, her heart pounding out of control. Her breaths came in short little pants, not from fear, but from a combination of adrenaline, emotion and shock. She still couldn't quite wrap her mind around what had just happened. She'd just had a conversation with... "That was Fat Lip Nathan."

Jared paused for one second, then nodded. "Uh-huh."

She'd interacted with a ghost. A real, live...er, *dead*...ghost. "He looked so solid. So alive."

"I know. And young. He sure didn't look like the old miser Marsden I knew growing up. Guess that was him in his heydey."

"He was very handsome," she admitted, her voice as shaky as her body. "I think I even understand why Hildy liked the whole lip thing."

Then she laughed, knowing she sounded slightly hysterical. God, what a surreal conversation to be having. The two of them were casually talking about the looks of a ghost.

Jared tenderly kissed her head, smoothing her hair back, still holding her close. Surprise over her unexpected encounter with the supernatural began to ease as she recognized the second chance she'd been given. Shock was quickly replaced by hope.

"So, was he right?" she asked, looking up at him, focusing on her present instead of another person's past. "Is a simple conversation going to make things work between us?"

Jared smiled. "It's a start. All I can tell you for sure is that I know I've fallen in love with you."

Her breath caught at his heartfelt words, but she had to try to think clearly. "It's too soon...." Yet even as she protested, she knew it was possible. Hadn't she, after all, done the same thing?

"Yeah. And slowing down, getting to know each other all over again, for real this time, is only going to make me love you more," he added. "*If* you'll let us try. Because, I've got to be honest with you, Gwen, I want nothing more than to stay here and try. Maybe my cousin Sophie was right about the kind of man I was five years ago, but not now.

Even before I met you, I'd realized just how much was missing from my life because of the way I've been living it." He cupped her face, tenderly stroking her cheek, as if memorizing the texture of her skin. "I know what I want, and it all revolves around you."

She nodded, believing, accepting. Understanding completely. "Well, *both* your cousins were wrong. Because Mick didn't understand me, either. Miles Stone, the adventurer, excited me at first, but the man...*you,* Jared Winchester...brought me to life. I want the guy who's afraid of heights. The one who drives fast when he's excited." She giggled. "The one who plays strip poker when he's already naked." She tilted her head back, looking into his dark brown eyes, willing him to believe every word. "I want *you.* I love you. I want nothing more than for you to stay until we figure out what's going to happen next."

He began to smile, then to laugh, and Gwen understood. Laughter spilled from her lips as well, spurred on by belief in the future, and a kind of deep-rooted happiness she'd never expected to find.

"Kiss me...*Jared.*"

He didn't hesitate, bending to meet her lips briefly, then again, and again, as if they were strangers kissing for the first time. Maybe, in some ways, they were. This was, after all, a new beginning.

They shared several soul-shattering kisses, and she wanted nothing more than to fall into the bed with him, to make love with him and whisper his real name while he was deep inside her body.

But there was one more thing to deal with first. "Jared, did you understand what Nathan meant when he mentioned my grandma?"

He kissed her temple, still holding her close, his fingers tangled in her hair. "Yeah, sweetheart. I understood."

She thought she did, too. Her gaze fell on the chair, where a small stack of old black-and-white photographs sat.

"You sure you're ready for that?" Jared asked, following her stare. He sounded as if he knew what she was going to find.

"Yes." Because she almost already knew, too. The word Nathan had used, that one little word—grandma—had stuck in her mind, repeating and repeating, taunting her to find out the truth. She walked over and picked up the photos. And when she saw the image of a very young Nathaniel Marsden, with his arm around a very young—and very pregnant—Hildy Compton, she understood at once.

"They're my grandparents," she whispered.

He walked over to join her, slipping a tender arm around her waist. "Yes."

She leaned her head on his shoulder. "I wonder if my father ever knew."

"He didn't," Jared replied. When she glanced up at him curiously, his expression was sad. "Hildy told me the story this morning. I think she knew what was going to happen and wanted me to be here to help you deal with it."

"Did she think I'd be angry? That finding out she's my grandmother would make me love her any less than I already do?" Gwen asked, stunned at the idea.

He shrugged. "Considering how her own parents and siblings treated her, she couldn't be sure. They took her baby while she was in prison, gave him to her older, married sister to raise. When she got out, they threatened that if she told anyone the truth, she'd never see him again. With the courts in those days, they were probably right."

A painful knot formed in Gwen's stomach, rising into her throat. It was too cruel to be believed. In spite of her brush with the law as a teenager, Hildy had always had a truly good heart. She'd been the most kindhearted, understanding, fun and generous person in Gwen's life.

And that sweet, zany woman had been denied her own son, and her granddaughter. "God, no wonder she had a breakdown. She lived a lie her entire adult life." Tears rose in Gwen's eyes, hot and sudden. "Why didn't Nathan do something?" she asked, wishing someone, somewhere along the line, had come to her grandmother's defense.

"He was in prison for forty years, Gwen." Though she didn't ask, he probably knew by her expression that she wanted to know more. He merely shook his head. "You can probably guess what for. By the time he got out and tracked down Hildy, she was older and afraid. You were a baby. She thought she'd be cut out of your life if she told your father or let Nathan tell him. So she sent Nathan away. He moved here, lived out his days alone. And she stayed in Boston. With you."

Her heart ached for Hildy and Nathan. She resolved, at that moment, to make Hildy's last years on this earth as happy as she possibly could. Which meant... "Are you thinking of writing a book about the history of organized crime? The gangster era?"

"I've often thought about it," he admitted. "But only if you and Hildy want me to."

She nodded once, not even having to think about her answer. "I do. If that's what she wants."

He gave her a kiss then, sweet, wet, and deep, telling her wordlessly that he'd do whatever he could to make her happy. She believed him. How could she not? He'd already made her happier than she'd ever imagined possible.

"I do have a favor to ask," she said when they broke apart.

"Yes?" he said, his eyes twinkling, as if he already knew what she was thinking.

He probably did.

"When you're working late on your book some night...can we dress up as bank robbers? Fake Tommy guns and all?"

He threw back his head and laughed, loud and long. "Babe, as long as we're together, we can do anything you want."

Epilogue

From the Chicago Travel Journal

LOOKING FOR A GOOD PLACE to mix in a little adventure with your relaxing vacation? Then don't miss the hottest, jazziest new bed-and-breakfast to open this side of a speakeasy. Check your calendars, pick up the phone and get on the waiting list for your own trip to The Little Bohemie Inn, in Derryville, Illinois.

The Little Bohemie opened just over two months ago, on Halloween weekend, with all the adventure, hijinks, ghostly shenanigans and just plain fun the holiday can provide. From the moment I arrived, I sensed my visit would be a memorable one. The ambience and historic furnishings, as well as the gothic appearance of the nineteenth-century era mansion, exude an almost palpable energy. The gangster theme is repeated again and again, from the names of each suite, to the cocktails offered every evening. My favorite was the Marcini Martini, a specialty of Miss Hildy Compton, co-owner of the inn.

Stepping inside the inn is like stepping into another era, another world. One might almost expect to round a corner and come face-to-face with a flapper on the arm of a high roller, or a dangerous bank robber hiding out from those daring G-men.

In The Little Bohemie, it feels as though anything can happen. Though I'm not a fanciful person, I found myself, on more than one occasion, feeling touched by another presence. As the house is rumored to be haunted, the ghostly ambience was particularly well suited to a Halloween trip.

The innkeepers, Gwen Compton and her aunt, were warm and gracious, and the service delightful, with minor touches that make a good guest house a great one. The cocktail hour hors d'ouevres were acceptable, but the true culinary masterpiece was Sunday morning's country breakfast.

Feeling compelled to determine if my delight in The Little Bohemie was attributable merely to the Halloween atmosphere—and a series of entertaining events which occurred during that initial visit—I made a return trip to the inn for the New Year's holiday. I am pleased to report that my next adventure proved every bit as entertaining as the first. The Little Bohemie's ambience and atmosphere are just as appealing when bedecked with garland and greenery as with witches and pumpkins.

I also count myself fortunate to have been in the Comptons' home to toast in the New Year, as well as to celebrate the recent engagement of Gwen Compton to well-known writer Jared Winchester. Miss Compton has informed me that she and her future husband will soon be offering a new, unique holiday experience. One weekend per month will be designated a "mystery holiday," where all registered guests arrive in character and attempt to solve a murder during their stay.

I already have my reservations for their first such weekend—set in the roaring twenties. Perhaps I'll see you there.

Until next time, this is your travel reviewer, Ricardo Tavares, wishing you many happy journeys.

* * * * *

Get to know Mick's sister, Sophie, as she tangles with
Derryville's new police chief, Daniel Fletcher.
Watch for their story
THRILL ME
in the January 2004 Harlequin collection
READ BETWEEN THE LINES

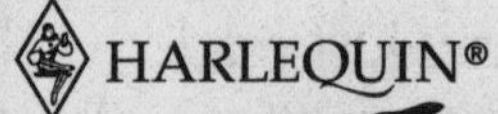

Temptation®

COMING NEXT MONTH

#949 IT'S ALL ABOUT EVE Tracy Kelleher
When tap pants go missing not once, but *three* times, lingerie-store owner Eve Cantoro calls in the cops. As soon as Carter Moran arrives, he hopes Eve will keep calling, and often! The chemistry between them is red-hot, and as events heat up at the shop, Eve's stock isn't the only lingerie that goes missing....

#950 UNDER FIRE Jamie Denton
Some Like It Hot, Bk. 3
OSHA investigator Jana Linney has never had really *good* sex. So when she meets sexy firefighter Ben Perry, she decides to do something about it. Having a one-night stand isn't like her, but if anyone can "help" her, Ben can. Only, one night isn't enough... and a repeat performance is unlikely, once Jana discovers she's investigating the death of one of Ben's co-workers. Still, now that Jana's tasted what sex *should* be, she's *not* giving it up....

#951 ONE NAUGHTY NIGHT Joanne Rock
The Wrong Bed—linked to Single in South Beach
Renzo Cesare has always been protective toward women. So it makes complete sense for him to "save" the beautiful but obviously out of her league Esmerelda Giles at a local nightclub. But it doesn't make sense for him to claim to be her blind date. He's not sure where *that* impulse came from. But before he can figure out a way to tell her the truth, she's got him in a lip lock so hot, he'll say anything to stay there!

#952 BARELY BEHAVING Jennifer LaBrecque
Heat
After three dead-end trips down the matrimonial highway, Tammy Cooper is giving up on marriage. She's the town bad girl—and she's proud of it. From now on, her motto is "Love 'em and leave 'em." Only, her plan takes a hit when gorgeous veterinarian Niall Fortson moves in next door. He's more than willing to let Tammy love him all she wants. But he's not letting her go anywhere....

HTCNM1003